HAUNTED HIGH TEA AND HOMICIDE

THE JANE AUSTEN TEAROOM MYSTERIES
BOOK 1

SUZY BUSSELL

Haunted High Tea and Homicide

The Jane Austen Tearoom Mysteries Book 1

By Suzy Bussell

This book and series is dedicated in loving memory of my mother, Erica.

CHAPTER 1

I hammered a nail into the wall, then picked up the large framed print of the most famous portrait of Jane Austen – the one with the blue dress and white lace cap – and hung it up. I stood back to admire it, hands on hips. Jane looked out over the till and souvenir section of my Regency-themed tearoom, the grand opening of which was in a few hours. Everything was almost in place.

"Well, Jane, what do you think? Will you keep watch over my new tearoom?" I asked her.

Jane didn't answer.

I looked at the far wall, where a portrait of Colin Firth as Mr Darcy sat judging me. "What about you, Fitzwilliam?"

Sadly, he said nothing either.

"Well, if you two won't help, I'll have to do it on my own."

I surveyed my tearoom. Almost everything seemed in order, and a thrill of excitement ran through me. My Regency-themed tearoom had been my everything for the last six months, and the blood, sweat and tears of getting to this moment were all worth it. It would open later today, and I expected a large crowd of friends and dignitaries from the town.

The town in question was Sidmouth, Devon, where I grew up. At eighteen, I had abandoned it for the bright lights of London, until I reached forty-two and my marriage broke down. So here I was, back in my real home, ready to start the next phase of my life.

My tearoom was decorated to sweep visitors into the charm of the Regency era. I had picked soft hues of cream and green throughout, with crisp white tablecloths edged in delicate lace. High-backed chairs, upholstered in period-appropriate patterns, circled the tables. Artworks, reminiscent of Jane Austen's narratives, were hung on the walls, enhancing the room's historical feel. In one cosy corner, a delightful display offered Regency-themed keepsakes and Jane Austen-inspired gifts, encouraging guests to take a piece of their experience home.

All the staff would be dressed in Regency costumes, including me. I'd had dresses made specially, and spent far too much time agonising over them. All my staff were women, but in time, I hoped to recruit at least one male to take on the persona of an Austen hero.

The tearoom was in a building sandwiched between two large hotels, halfway along the esplanade and facing the sea, with the main road in front. It was a prime spot, with high rent. But as soon as it became vacant, I knew I had to have it.

I took my notebook from my apron pocket and checked the to-do list. I'd done everything on it, and now all I had to do was wait for the guests to arrive.

There was a crash from the kitchen. I hurried in to find my best friend and closest confidante, Holly, picking up cucumber sandwiches from the floor. She'd volunteered to help out today to make sure everything went smoothly. "Sorry about the noise." She sighed. "I knocked over one of the trays. These will all have to go in the bin. I'll make some more." Holly didn't have to bend far to pick up the scattered sandwiches, being just over five feet tall. A stark contrast to me at five foot eleven.

I bent to help. "Don't worry, I can do it. Don't you have to drop Jacob off at the childminder?"

"He's already there. I'm all yours until five."

I looked warmly at Holly. "I'm so grateful you're here. It means the world to me, especially knowing how busy you are in your craft shop." Then I looked at her clothes: blue jeans and a floaty black top, with her long, blonde hair loose. "Aren't you going to change into a Regency frock?"

She screwed up her nose. "I don't think any of them will fit."

She was probably right. Throughout our friendship, which had started when we were eleven, we'd never been able to share clothes, and the Regency dresses I had made were for women at least a few inches taller.

I picked up one of the silver trays of sandwiches, and we went back to the tearoom. I put the tray on the long table set up for the food, now groaning with cakes, sandwiches and scones, all samples from my menu. I had spent months agonising over it all and had given everything names linked to Austen. Darcy's Devonshire Cream Tea, Mansfield Park Mini Quiches, Persuasion's Cornish Pasties, Anne Elliot's Almond Slices and Mrs Bennet's Bath Buns were just a a few of them.

"Try not to worry," said Holly. "Everything will go swimmingly, and you'll have fretted over nothing."

I laughed. "Reading my mind again."

"Always."

My anxiety levels had been sky-high these last few weeks. Sometimes I wondered why, at forty-two years old, I was starting from scratch after years of working in other people's cafés and restaurants. I was finally branching out on my own after years of telling myself I would one day, but never doing it. If it hadn't been for Holly and my Aunt Ruby's encouragement, I would have given up.

"How many did you say you were expecting?" Holly asked, eyeing the table.

"About forty."

"If it gets too crowded in here, I'll guide some of them into the tea garden."

The walled tea garden at the back was another reason I had chosen this location. Behind the main building, it was big enough for five tables on the lawn and felt like a secret tucked away from the bustle of the esplanade.

Holly disappeared into the kitchen just as Carol and Emma, my staff, arrived at the front door. They waved and I unlocked the door to let them in. "Come in. I think we're almost ready."

They were both dressed in their Regency costumes. Carol's short grey hair was covered by a lace cap, and her high-waisted, floor-length cotton gown had a small flower pattern, with a high lace neckline that matched the cap.

Emma, who was nineteen, wore a light-blue cotton dress with an empire waistline, short puffed sleeves and a low, square neckline. Her hair was in an elegant up-do, gathered into a bun with soft tendrils framing her face.

I clapped my hands together. "You both look fabulous. This is going to be a fantastic day! Come on. I'll show you what you need to do." I led them to the buffet table, then into the kitchen, giving them instructions for the afternoon.

It was five minutes to three when I unlocked the door and turned the sign to Open. Then I walked to the counter, reached underneath to the sound system and pressed play. The soundtrack to the 1993 BBC production of *Pride and Prejudice* filled the room. Everything was perfect.

The first guests arrived ten minutes later. I welcomed them at the door and directed them to the buffet table, where Carol stood ready to serve.

The town's mayor, Edward Whitaker, arrived soon after and shook my hand. A rotund man in his sixties, he wore his mayoral chains over a grey suit.

"Thank you so much for agreeing to cut the ribbon," I said, smiling.

"My pleasure." He looked around the room. "What a delightful place. The tourists will love it."

"I hope so. And the locals, too."

"So what's the plan today?"

"A brief speech by me at four o'clock, and if you would like to give one, too, you're very welcome. Then you'll cut the ribbon and we'll take photos."

"Sounds perfect."

More guests came through the door. "Carol will give you a cup of tea," I said, indicating her.

He leaned towards me. "There isn't anything stronger than tea, is there?"

I laughed. "No! I need a licence to sell alcohol, as you well know." Maybe one day I would get one and serve Prosecco afternoon teas, but for now, I was sticking to alcohol-free.

"You're not selling it today; you're giving it away. Don't worry, I've brought a flask." He patted his inside jacket pocket and winked.

The flow of arrivals eased, so I mingled with the guests, most of whom had already helped themselves to food and drink and sat down at a table. Many complimented me on the tearoom and my Regency costume. I'd chosen my best dress for the opening: a ballgown, with a high empire waist that emphasised my tall figure and a flowing, floor-length skirt made from dark-red satin. The low neckline, short puffed sleeves and delicate embellishments added to its splendour. I'd coaxed my long, brown hair into a bun and added a sparkling comb with red crystals to match the dress.

A chime from the bell above the front door announced two more guests: Heather and Susan from the Sidmouth Business

Consortium, a local hub for business owners and entrepreneurs to network and advance their shared interests. The consortium held weekly meetings, workshops and community events.

"Heather, Susan, so lovely to see you both! I was worried you'd miss the start," I said as I made my way over, careful not to trip on my hem.

"Wouldn't miss it for the world," Heather replied, looking around the tearoom with an approving eye. "I have to say, it's an absolute dream. Just like stepping back in time." Heather, in her early fifties, had only a few silver strands in her honey-brown hair. She was always impeccably dressed and made up. Today she wore a soft cashmere sweater with a flowing skirt. I wished I could look so effortlessly attractive.

"And she can't resist a good scone," Susan chimed in, her laughter mingling with the tinkling of china and the murmuring of guests. Susan was in her sixties, and her grey pixie cut matched her dark-blue trouser suit.

I looked around. The guests were enjoying the food and drink and everything was going as planned. And boy, had I planned! It was even better than I'd hoped. I felt a warm rush of happiness and smiled at the portrait of Jane Austen. Surely Jane would approve, and my tearoom would be an unmitigated success. All that was missing was my son Oliver. I missed him dreadfully already, and hoped he was getting on all right at university.

A few minutes later, my mirth was dampened. A familiar tall man with greying hair walked in, accompanied by a woman.

Oh no, what's he *doing here?*

CHAPTER 2

I recognised the man only too well. It was Larry Cunningham, the chairman of Sidmouth Business Consortium, with his wife, Debbie. Larry was the last person I'd expected to turn up, even though I'd invited him.

I hurried to the other side of the tearoom where Holly was handing out canapés. "Larry Cunningham's here," I whispered.

Holly's eyes darted around the room, looking for him. "What the...? But he's spent the last few months trying to stop your tearoom from opening."

"I know!" I recalled Larry's objections, not just to the council's planning committee but also via derogatory social media posts designed to provoke opposition from the town. Luckily, the council and the rest of the town hadn't agreed with him, and most thought a Regency-themed tearoom would be a great addition. "Do you think he's had a change of heart?"

Holly snorted. "I doubt it."

"So he's here to cause trouble?"

"Probably. Although he's brought his wife. Maybe she's persuaded him to come and be nice." Holly took a Bingley's bite-size Yorkshire pudding with roast beef and horseradish canapé off the tray and popped it in her mouth.

Larry walked over to the buffet table and inspected it. Debbie trailed meekly in his wake, with an apologetic smile.

Carol poured Larry a cup of tea and he took it, with a plate of sandwiches and two scones, to a table at the side of the room. Debbie followed him with a cup of tea and sat down.

Susan sidled over. "Look what the cat brought in," she said in a dry tone.

"Surprised to see him here," Heather added. "He's as stubborn as a mule, that one."

I shrugged. "Well, it means a lot that you're here to support me. I'm going to tackle the problem head-on. Wish me luck."

I walked over to Larry and Debbie. "Mr Cunningham. I wasn't expecting you."

Larry looked up at me. "I decided to see your new venture for myself. I thought it would be bad, but this is ridiculous." He looked me up and down in my Regency gown, then put a whole finger sandwich in his mouth and chewed, still staring at me. I looked at Debbie, who smiled and gave a tiny shrug.

I took a moment to compose myself, then addressed Larry again. "As you can see, Larry, the whole town has come to support the start of my adventure. And I'm glad you could come, too."

"Well, you've piqued my curiosity. Maybe there's more to this venture than meets the eye. But I'll be keeping a close eye on your progress. This town has plenty of tourists, but when they've gone home during the winter, you'll struggle. I've said it before, and I'll say it again: there are too many cafés in this town already."

"Ah, but there aren't any Regency-themed tearooms. And Sidmouth is a Regency seaside town, made famous when the Prince Regent visited."

"Why all the Jane Austen things, then?"

"Jane Austen visited Sidmouth, too, in 1801. Reportedly, she fell in love here."

Larry didn't look convinced, and I wondered whether Bath or Lyme Regis would have been a better place to open. But Sidmouth was popular. In the summer months it was heaving with tourists, all attracted to the beautiful beach, the Regency architecture, and the quiet, non-tacky shops and cafés. "Let's make a deal," I said. "If I'm still here in a year's time, you'll make a public apology to me. Deal?" I extended my hand for him to shake.

Larry contemplated it for a moment. "I don't make deals," he said in a stern tone. I withdrew my hand and closed my eyes in exasperation.

I was saved by a familiar voice behind me. "Trinity!"

Aunt Ruby had arrived, fashionably late as ever. Slender and tall, with short silver-grey hair styled in a funky, unconventional way, she wore an elegant midi-dress with an abstract floral design, a soft waistline, and tasteful embellishments.

"You're here!" I kissed my aunt on the cheek.

"Better late than never. So, what's this all about?" She indicated Larry.

I took my aunt's arm and guided her to the buffet table. "He's here to criticise, so I tried to turn it around." I told her about the bet I'd tried to make.

"And he wouldn't agree to it?"

"No, but I'm determined to make sure I'm in business for many years to come."

Aunt Ruby picked up a cream- and jam-spread scone and took a bite. "He's a horrible man. I should have known he'd turn up, probably for the free food."

"Actually, I invited him. I thought that if he could see the tearoom in all its glory, he'd be won over. How wrong I was.

Now I have to put up with him. I hope he doesn't upset the other guests."

Aunt Ruby looked around the room. "Well, I wouldn't have invited him. When you get to my age, you'll realise horrible men like him are best kept at arm's length. If not further."

We watched Larry stand up, take his empty plate to the buffet table, fill it, then go into the garden.

"Let's hope he stays out there," Aunt Ruby said. "Oh look, there's Mary. I need to speak to her about the art display next month." She hurried to the other side of the room.

I went over to Carol at the food table. "How is everything?" I asked her, surveying the table. "They've made a dent in the food. Do you think I should get some extra scones out?"

Carol smiled, looking at the throng of people. "I don't think so. It won't be long until the ceremony, and then everyone's bound to start drifting off." She looked at me. "Get yourself a cup of tea and breathe for a moment. Enjoy the day. Look at everyone who's come to wish you well."

She had a point. I'd been so busy flitting around that I hadn't had time to stand back and take it all in. It really was a sight to see. Finally, everything was falling into place.

Fifteen minutes later, after helping myself to a cup of tea and a scone or two, I was chatting to guests and thinking about starting the opening ceremony, when I felt a hand on my arm. "Come quickly," muttered Holly. "There's a row in the garden."

My mind raced through a hundred different scenarios. I dashed outside and saw Larry facing off with another man I didn't recognise. Their faces were inches apart as they shouted at each other.

"I'm not talking to you." Larry pointed his finger at the other man's face.

"You're not going to get away with it again!" the other man bellowed.

"The police have nothing to prosecute!" Larry shouted back. "If you're not careful, I'll get a restraining order put on you!"

"A restraining order on me! You're the one who needs a restraining order. You're disgusting. Everyone needs to know!"

The other man grabbed Larry's shirt and a sort-of fight started. Both men were in their late sixties at best, so it was more of a scuffle than an actual fight. Larry's reach was longer, but he was thin, whereas the other man was stocky.

This had the potential to ruin my opening. If I didn't put a stop to it now, the fight would be all anyone would talk about afterwards.

Not one to shy away from confrontation, I dived in and pulled the two men apart by their upper arms. "Stop it! This is my opening event, and I'm not having it ruined by you two."

I turned to the other man. "I don't know what this is about, but I didn't invite you. Who are you?"

"He's a bloody nuisance; that's who he is," Larry shouted.

The other man panted, his face red. He glared at Larry, then looked at me. "My apologies. I only came here to confront this dreadful man. He's a disgrace to humanity." He leaned around me to bellow at Larry. "You've not heard the last of me!" Then he released himself from my grip and went into the tearoom.

There was a general hum of talking as the guests exclaimed over what had just happened. I felt my face flush.

"Sorry about that, everyone," I said. "Carry on."

I stood in the middle of the garden, scarcely able to believe what had just transpired. I considered throwing Larry out, too, but decided it would cause less fuss to leave him be. I looked over at him. He was sitting at a table opposite Debbie, looking flustered. He flexed his shoulders, then picked up his cup and drained it.

Stupid man. I wish he'd stayed at home. I shouldn't have invited him.

I decided to go into the tearoom and check that the other man had left. I looked around but couldn't see him. I breathed a sigh of relief. I wanted things to go off with a bang, but not like this.

Time to get the opening ceremony done. That should bring everyone back to the event's purpose. I tapped the side of a glass with a teaspoon to get their attention. My hands were shaking a little: the kerfuffle in the garden had affected me more than I thought. "Good afternoon, everyone," I said loudly. "If you'd like to gather round…"

Guests filed in from the tea garden. The room fell silent, and a sea of faces gazed at me. This was the moment I'd been waiting for. My own project, my own business, was about to begin. No more working for other people: people who took me for granted, people who didn't value me.

I cleared my throat. "Thank you all for coming today. It's wonderful to have you all here, sharing in my happiness at the opening of my Regency tearoom. I don't want any cakes, scones, or sandwiches left over, so please keep eating."

"Don't worry, Trinity," a voice called. "Your scones are more sought after than Mr Darcy at a ball."

Laughter filled the room.

"When I conceived the idea for this tearoom, I never thought it would actually happen," I continued. "As my Aunt Ruby can confirm, I've adored Jane Austen since I was fifteen. Coming to work every day to immerse myself in her world fills me with joy. Spread the word, and I hope to see all of you as regulars soon. Now, let's welcome the mayor, Edward Whitaker, who will cut the ribbon."

Polite applause followed. I scanned the crowd for Larry, relieved not to see him.

Edward stepped up. "It's an absolute pleasure to be here. I wish Miss Bishop all the best with this new addition to the town."

Carol handed me one end of a red ribbon. Edward cut it. Phones were raised for photos, more applause followed and then people started to dissipate.

Several people congratulated me before Debbie rushed over. "I'm so sorry for the earlier disturbance in the garden," she whispered.

"It wasn't your fault, Debbie. What was it about?"

"That man is Larry's old business partner, David." She talked so quietly that I had to bend down and put my ear close to her face.

"Does he live nearby?"

"No," she said, offering no more details.

"What were they fighting over?"

"I'd rather not say." She shuddered. "I tried to persuade Larry to stay home. When he's made up his mind, there's no changing it."

As I nodded, thinking there was nothing I could do about it now, a scream pierced the air. It came from the garden. All conversation halted.

Someone rushed inside. "There's a man in the garden and he's dead!"

CHAPTER 3

Barely comprehending the words, a wave of panic flooded over me as I went outside. *Surely they must be joking*. Debbie followed me, and we both froze, mouths open in amazement.

Debbie pointed at Larry. He was at the same table as before, slumped facedown in a plate of food.

I moved closer and saw one of my own cake knives sticking out between Larry's shoulder blades. Blood had seeped from the wound.

"Oh my goodness!" I gasped. It took a moment to fully grasp what I was looking at.

"He's dead!" A woman shouted behind me.

I turned and saw more people coming into the garden. Then I moved forward and felt for a pulse on his neck. There was nothing.

"Who would do such a thing?" a man cried, and there was a general hubbub of noise.

"Everyone, step back," I said. "We need to make sure we don't contaminate the crime scene." I'd watched enough police dramas and mysteries to know that any forensic evidence must be preserved.

Aunt Ruby pushed her way to the front. "Is he really dead?"

"Yes. We need to call the police."

"I'll do it." Aunt Ruby pulled out her phone and dialled 999. "Police, please. There's been a murder…"

———

The ambulance crew arrived first. They checked Larry for signs of life and confirmed he was dead. A few minutes later, four police officers entered the tearoom. Three were in uniform, one in plain clothes: a dark-grey suit, black shirt and black tie. The grey would have made some men look drab but his olive skin glowed. He had black hair, with a significant amount of stubble that wasn't quite a beard.

"I'm DI O'Malley," he said, in a thick Irish brogue. "We've had a report of a murder here."

I stepped forward. "I'm the owner, and yes, there has been a murder."

"And you are?" He looked me up and down, taking in my unusual attire.

"Trinity Bishop."

"Is there a Regency ball I wasn't invited to?" Then he added more seriously, "Can you show me the body?"

I nodded.

He turned to one of the uniformed officers. "Smith, get everyone's name and contact details. Don't let anyone leave until we've spoken to them."

There were a few groans from the rest of the guests.

I led DI O'Malley to the garden; the other two officers followed.

I stayed by the door and watched the detective talk to the ambulance crew. Once they'd finished talking, he came over. "Do you know who this man is?"

"His name is Larry Cunningham. He's the chairman of

Sidmouth Business Consortium. His wife, Debbie, was here, too. She's inside, and in shock, so she's being looked after." Carol had taken charge of Debbie.

He nodded. "I'll need to speak to you all, of course. Who discovered him?"

"I don't know. I was in the tearoom and we heard a scream."

"All right. Please wait inside with the others: I'll talk to you soon." He went back to the other officers.

Aunt Ruby came up behind me and tapped my arm. "That DI is very handsome," she whispered in my ear.

I gasped. "Aunt Ruby! A man has been murdered in my tearoom, and all you can think about is how good-looking the detective is?"

Aunt Ruby pursed her lips, a glint in her eye. "I wonder if he's single…"

I shook my head. "There's no way he's single. He's drop-dead gorgeous." Then I shook myself. "I can't believe we're discussing the detective's dating prospects when there's been a murder. Then again, if he's as good at solving crimes as he is at looking good, we'll find the killer in no time."

Twenty minutes later, things were getting rowdy. Although a murder had taken place, the remaining guests were becoming fractious.

One by one, they were questioned, then allowed to leave, but not before they'd given their personal details.

I sat watching the police officers work. Every customer was asked whether they'd seen the murder or noticed anyone near Larry at around the time he had been stabbed. They also asked each customer if they'd observed anyone acting suspiciously.

I tried to remember what I'd seen, but came up with nothing. What I recalled was that after the fight with his ex-business partner, Larry hadn't been in the audience when I was making my speech. Shortly afterwards, he'd been found stabbed. Did that mean he had been murdered during the opening ceremony?

Who had been in the room? I remembered my aunt, my friend Holly and a few others. Some people had recorded the opening on their phones. Hopefully, the police could pick up on who had been in the room by watching that. But even if a person had been in the room, it was no guarantee that they hadn't done it. They could have slipped out and done the deed while I was talking.

When Aunt Ruby had given her statement, she came over. "I'll stay as long as you want me to."

"Thanks, but you might as well go. There's no point in hanging around. Do you think they'll take the body away soon?" The forensic team had already arrived and the pathologist.

"I can't imagine they'd keep him here any longer than they have to."

Two hours later, everyone had gone except me, the police and the CSI team. A female police officer had taken Debbie home. She had sat rigid as a statue for ages. I wanted to change out of my Regency costume. Despite not wearing a corset, I longed for a pair of sweatpants and a T-shirt. How any woman wore this getup all the time, I couldn't fathom. Despite my fascination with the Regency period, I thanked my lucky stars I hadn't been alive back then.

I was sitting at the table near the till when DI O'Malley came over and sat down beside me. Now it was my turn to be questioned.

CHAPTER 4

O'Malley had the darkest brown eyes I'd ever seen. "So, Miss Bishop?" he said, in his thick Irish accent.

"Call me Trinity."

He ran his hand through his hair. It was very endearing. Maybe the gesture was intended to lower my defences before he questioned me. A new police technique, hire only really handsome men, so that witnesses and potential suspects can't help spilling the beans.

"Can you tell me everything that happened today in your own words, please?" He gave me a boyish smile and looked at me as if he was really interested in what I had to say. I tried my best not to be affected by that look. It was difficult. Despite such feelings being highly inappropriate, especially since a corpse had just been removed, I couldn't help noticing his perfectly formed nose, or losing myself in the darkness of his eyes. It was almost hypnotic.

"Everything? From what time?"

"When you got here."

"I got here at about six am and spent the morning preparing for the opening. Carol and Emma arrived at nine to help."

"They're your staff?"

"Yes. Holly came to help at around one. She owns the craft shop next door. Then, at three, the guests started arriving."

"When did Mr Cunningham, the victim, arrive?"

"I can't say for sure, but it noticed him about half past three."

"Did you speak to him?"

"Yes. I went over to him and we spoke briefly."

"Had you invited him to the event?"

"You mean did he gatecrash? I take it you've heard we didn't get on."

O'Malley executed a sort of one-shouldered shrug.

"I invited him, yes. He was always opposed to my tearoom. He said the town didn't need yet another café. But I wanted him to see how different this one was. It's not a café; it's a tearoom. They're very different things."

O'Malley listened patiently, staring intently at me. "So what happened when he arrived?"

"We chatted. He said he'd only come to be nosey and see what all the fuss was about. He helped himself to a lot of food, so I think he came for a free meal, too."

O'Malley sat back in his chair. "So you didn't hear him tell half the garden that he had no intention of ever apologising to you, and in fact, would do all he could to get you closed down?"

I did a double-take. "What?"

"You didn't hear it?"

"No! He was going to try and wreck my tearoom?" Anger rose inside me. "Stupid man." What a cheek! All the time he'd been at my opening, he'd been planning to do goodness knows what to close me down. He really was beyond the pale.

DI O'Malley cleared his throat. "How much did you speak to him outside of Sidmouth Business Consortium? You're a member, I see." He looked at the small plaque with the SBC logo, near the till.

"I am a member, yes, but I've only been to a couple of meetings so far. I've been too busy setting up the tearoom."

"At how many meetings did you speak to him?"

I thought back. "Two. Both times he said he opposed the tearoom. After the second time, I avoided him like the plague."

O'Malley looked around him. "I take it you're a Jane Austen fan? Jane Austen gifts, Jane Austen-themed items on the menu and pictures of all the major Austen heroes from the adaptations." There was a hint of a smile on his face.

"*Fan* doesn't even begin to describe it. I've loved her books since I was fifteen. She isn't just an author; she's a timeless voice, a friend. I love her because she mastered the art of subtlety and wit. She says so much about society and human nature in her books. Reading her works is like stepping back into the Regency era, a delightful escape from modern life. And let's not forget the romance, quiet but powerful, always there in the background. No explosions of emotion, just steady, growing love." I looked around the tearoom. "It's taken so much work to get the tearoom ready for the grand opening."

Now, crushing thoughts of what the murder might mean for my business flooded in. I'd planned for everything – renovation problems, staff illness, food-supply issues... I had insurance for everything. But murder in my tearoom? No one could plan for that.

"Was anyone else opposed to the tearoom?"

"No one I knew. There were a couple of comments on social media, but there's always someone. Larry was in the minority. Only a few people in the town objected: everyone else has been supportive."

He picked up his pen and started playing with it. "So was there any other reason why you two didn't get on?"

My eyes narrowed. "Are you fishing for a motive?"

A smile played on the detective's lips, but he said nothing. I wondered what was so funny. Of course, I was a suspect, like everyone else. But it still stung. Though I now despised Larry even more for his comments, I would never have murdered him. But I suppose DI O'Malley didn't know that.

"As I said, I had no other contact with him apart from a few brief conversations at the SBC."

O'Malley didn't answer but wrote in his notebook. That was frustrating. Being dyslexic, I find reading difficult and especially reading handwriting, let alone reading something written upside down. Until I discovered Jane Austen, I'd always found reading novels unpleasant and torturous.

When the detective finished writing, he put his pen down and looked up at me. His gaze was appraising, but I didn't feel uncomfortable. He was probably deciding whether I was the murderer. Well, I had at least thirty different witnesses who'd watched my every move all afternoon. A shiver ran through me. *What a horrible thought.*

"We'll need your clothing for analysis," he said, eyeing my dress.

I stared at him. "You're looking for blood spatters?"

"It's routine. Do you have something you can change into?"

"Er, yeah. I have another five dresses just like this one. And normal clothes, obviously."

"In that case, please could you get changed and give the dress to the CSI team?"

I got up. "Okay."

"I don't have any other questions for now." He reached into his inside jacket pocket and gave me his card. "If you think of anything important, anything at all, call me. I'll be the detective in modern clothes."

I took the card and glanced at it. *DI Cormac O'Malley*, I read.

"Forensics will need to undertake further analysis of the whole tearoom."

"What? I can't reopen? The murder was in the gardens not in here."

"It'll only be for a day or two."

"But I've been planning the opening for months. I've worked nonstop for weeks." I sank into a chair and put my head in my hands. The opening was turning out exactly as Larry Cunningham had wanted – a complete disaster. Perversely, he was the reason behind it. If he wasn't dead, he'd be laughing at me.

O'Malley spoke again, more softly. "I understand it must be frustrating, but a man has been murdered, and we need to find out who did it. You'll be able to open once they've finished. I'll ask them to work as quickly as possible."

I looked up and nodded. Nothing could have prepared me for this. A murder in my tearoom, and it hadn't even officially opened yet. I'd been naïve to think this was ever going to work. All my hopes and dreams invested in this one thing, and for what?

The irony was that Larry had already won the bet. How would my tearoom survive such a scandal? No one would want to come and have tea and scones at a brutal-murder scene.

CHAPTER 5

A few hours later, I sat on Aunt Ruby's sofa, nursing a cup of tea and feeling very sorry for myself.

When the police had all left for the night, I'd given in to my aunt's pleading, packed some clothes and left my home: a two-bedroom semi in the heart of Sidmouth, to stay with her. Aunt Ruby lived a short walk away from the tearoom, in a row of modern terraced houses near the river Sid.

Aunt Ruby took a sip of her glass of Malbec. "Well, my dear, what a horrible situation this is."

"Tell me about it." I didn't have the energy to explain everything that had gone through my mind since seeing Larry Cunningham's dead body in my tea garden. I should have been preparing for the shop's first day of trading. Instead, I didn't know when my tearoom would reopen, if ever. Not to mention the dead body.

"I can believe that plenty of people wanted Larry dead," said Aunt Ruby. "He was a nasty, spiteful man. But actually murdering him? Wanting somebody dead that desperately is just terrible."

I nodded. I hadn't been so disheartened for a long time.

Not since I'd left my husband, in fact. It had taken me months to be happy again. Now it had all come crashing down, and I felt as if I were trapped in a bad dream. "Do you think the police will find out who did it?"

"Let's hope so. Otherwise, the gossips will have a field day."

"And my tearoom will be famous not for its excellent service and Regency theme, but because a man was murdered in my garden."

"Yes, that is rather unfortunate." Aunt Ruby paused. "You know what you should do?"

"What?"

"Find the killer yourself."

I goggled at my aunt. "How would I do that? I'm not a police officer."

"No, but you know most of the people who were at your opening ceremony, and you can do some digging to help the police. If you find the murderer quickly, the gossip around your tearoom will go away."

There was some truth in that. The sooner the case was solved, the sooner everything would be back to normal. Then I could reopen my tearoom and live the dream I'd wanted for so long.

"I'm just worried that no one will want to visit a tearoom where someone was stabbed."

"Or people might want to see where the crime happened."

"Do you think so? What sort of person would want to do that?"

Aunt Ruby shrugged. "There's all sorts of people in this world, Trinity, as you well know."

I nodded, thinking back to my twenty-plus years in London. It had been a culture shock when I arrived, a naïve eighteen-year-old from a small Devon town. I'd met all sorts of people there. But never anyone who'd want to visit the scene of a murder.

———

The next morning, I meandered home. My house, one of many two-bed Victorian terraces, was in the middle of the town: I'd bought it with my half of the money from the sale of the London house. Dean, my ex-husband, had bought a flat in Ealing. It hadn't taken long for me to decide to put the money I had left over into opening a Jane Austen-themed tearoom.

I picked up the post and went into the kitchen. There were several pieces of junk mail and a square brown parcel, smaller than my palm.

I turned it over. It must have been hand-delivered because there was no stamp or address, just my name: Trinity Bishop. Someone had packed it well, so it took me a few goes to penetrate the tape and open it.

Inside was a dark-blue velvet jewellery box, faded in the corners, with a worn-looking gold button. I opened it to find a gold ring with a single turquoise stone. I took out the ring and inspected it. "That's peculiar."

I examined the brown-paper packaging for a note, or something that might indicate who it was from. There was nothing. Even more strange, it looked exactly like Jane Austen's famous ring: gold, with a single turquoise stone. That ring was in Jane Austen's house: Chawton House, in Wiltshire. I knew all about it because years ago I'd contributed to a crowd funder to stop it from leaving the country when a wealthy buyer had tried to export it.

Maybe someone had sent it as a gift for the opening of the tearoom. Or maybe they wanted me to stock the rings in the tearoom shop, and this was a sample. Yes, that was probably it.

"It's lovely." It looked too small for my fingers, but I tried it on my ring finger, now empty.

Instead of stopping halfway as I expected, the ring went

straight on. "Oh!" I held my hand out to admire it. Then I felt a strange tingling all over my my body.

"Hello," said a voice behind me.

I gasped and spun round.

There stood not one, but five figures. They were all dressed in Regency outfits and they were all transparent. They looked like some sort of 3-D projection.

"What the…" I murmured.

A man with a mop of dark curly hair stepped forward. He was dressed in a Regency-era British army uniform: red coat, white breeches and black boots. He held up his hand. "Remain calm, madam. I understand this may be somewhat unexpected, but I entreat you to listen."

"W-who are you, and what are you doing in my house?" I managed to say.

The man sighed and rolled his eyes. "Always the same questions with each new owner."

One of the other figures, an old woman dressed in a dark-red gown with a matching red hat, spoke. "Get on with it, man. Do you want to scare her half to death?"

"Sorry. Where was I? Ah, yes." He bowed. "Lieutenant Geoffrey Wickers, at your service, ma'am." He clicked his heels together.

I stepped backwards and encountered the wall. I stared at the ring on my finger and pulled it off.

The people disappeared.

"Oh my God." I took a deep breath and dropped the ring on the counter as though it were red hot. Everything was quiet except for the sound of my breathing.

I moved to the place where the people had been and waved my arms, trying to see if there was something there, even though, of course, there wasn't. I turned around, checking they weren't behind me.

"I'm going mad," I said, under my breath. "Mad." It must be all the stress of yesterday.

I put the kettle on, took a mug out of the cupboard and made myself a nice cup of tea. I took a sip, eyeing the ring on the counter.

Then I prodded the ring. I looked around. Nothing.

I picked up the ring again. "Either I'm mad, or this ring is enchanted."

I put the ring on my finger, and the figures materialised before me as if fading in from the edges of reality.

"Don't take the ring off again," one of the other men said, pointing at my hand.

"Who are you? What are you?" I looked around the room, then up at the ceiling. My heart pounded in my chest.

"What are you looking for?" Geoffrey Wickers asked me.

"For a projector. This has to be some kind of joke."

"We are not from a projector," the old lady said, in a stern voice. "We are ghosts."

CHAPTER 6

"G-ghosts?" I stammered.

"Yes, ghosts. And don't even think about taking that ring off. It's highly inconvenient and also rude."

I stared at her and said in a slow, unsure tone. "He's already asked me not to. There's no need to keep repeating yourself. I'm not stupid."

The woman puckered her lips, clearly not used to being answered back. "We can only appear when someone wears that ring."

"Okaaay."

"The ring is enchanted. We are tied to it, and it to us."

I suppressed a nervous laugh. This was ridiculous. "So I can only see you when I wear the ring?"

"Yes."

"What happens to you when I take it off?"

"We are still here. We can't go far from the ring, but you can't see us."

"I'm going mad"—I ran my hands through my hair—"or you're all lying."

A man stepped forward. "You're not mad, and Lady

Camilla Du Borg would never lie. Would you, ma'am?" He was dressed in clergyman's clothes: black jacket, black breeches and a white shirt with a dog collar. He also wore a simpering expression.

Lady Camilla waved a dismissive hand at him. "Mr Collingwood, that is quite enough of your flattery for today."

"Mr Collingwood? Lady Camilla Du Borg?" I looked from one to the other. "Your names are very familiar. Well, almost."

A young girl at the back giggled. She looked about fifteen and was dressed in a sprigged muslin gown. She stepped forward and curtseyed. "Miss Lily Barrett."

I laughed and pointed to the ghost not yet introduced, a tall young man with a disapproving expression. "And I suppose your name is something like Mr Darcy?"

Lady Camilla lifted her chin in a disapproving way. "That is my nephew, Mr Fitzroy Darby."

I let out a belly laugh. The ghosts looked at me disapprovingly while I struggled to control myself. Eventually, I managed it. "This is a joke."

"A joke? By whom?" Mr Darby snapped, looking down his nose at me.

I stared at him. "I don't know. My friend Holly, maybe? My ex-husband? Someone who wants a laugh at my expense. Is this like one of those virtual reality headsets, except it projects out?"

Mr Darby stepped forward. "I can assure you, madam, that we are no joke. We are ghosts, and our names... Well, they will be familiar if you have read that awful book by Miss Jane Austen."

My eyes narrowed. No one calls Jane Austen awful on my watch. "You mean *Pride and Prejudice*? One of the best novels that's ever been written?"

He scoffed and folded his arms. "You are clearly not well-read."

"I am, actually. I may not have a degree in English literature, but I've read a lot of books and Jane Austen's are the best."

Lily giggled and Lady Camilla nudged her. "Shush, child."

"All right, let's say that you *are* actually ghosts. Why do you only appear when I put the ring on?"

Geoffrey Wickers opened his mouth, but a knock interrupted him. We all stared at each other.

I moved to take the ring off, but Lady Camilla shook her head. "No one else can see us. You don't need to take off the ring."

I went to answer the door, and my heart skipped a beat when I opened it and saw DI O'Malley. Then dread took over when I realised he might be here to arrest me. My mind flicked through a thousand images of myself being arrested, brought to trial, then banged up in prison.

"Hello. How can I help you?"

The corner of his mouth twitched. He was alone, so the chances of him arresting me seemed slimmer. "Hello to you, too. I stopped by to see how you are, now that you're back home."

I cast a furtive glance at the ghosts standing a few feet away, then opened the door wider and DI O'Malley stepped inside.

I led the way to the lounge. "That's very thoughtful of you."

"He's very handsome," said Lily, close by. "He sounds Irish." I turned, and realised all the ghosts had followed us into the lounge. At least DI O'Malley didn't seem to have heard anything.

I pretended to cough. "Yes."

O'Malley's brow furrowed. "Yes?"

"Er, yes, I'm back home."

I indicated the sofa, and we both sat down. He looked

around the room. "This is a nice house. Have you been here long?"

"Nearly six months."

"You grew up in Sidmouth, I believe."

"You've been doing your homework. Yes. I lived in London for just over twenty years."

"Ask the poor man if he wants tea," Lady Camilla scolded. "It's vulgar not to offer. Most inhospitable."

I looked over at her, floating in front of the TV. *Maybe it isn't a prank. Maybe they really are ghosts.* But it was the middle of the day. *Don't ghosts appear at night?*

I turned to O'Malley, avoiding eye contact. "Would you like some tea?"

He gave me a small smile. "No, thank you. I can't stay long."

"Rude not to accept," Fitzroy Darby muttered. "Even if he didn't want it, he should have accepted."

I silently agreed with him but changed the subject. "Do you know when I can open the tearoom?"

He smiled. "They'll finish later today, I think, and then you can go back in and open when you like. I know it must be annoying for you, but we need to make sure we get all the evidence."

"Yes, definitely Irish." Mr Collingwood went right up to O'Malley and peered into his face. O'Malley didn't flinch. Maybe the ghosts were right and only I could see them. I glanced at the ring. It wasn't glowing, sparkling, or showing any other sign of being some sort of ghost projector.

I tried to look as innocent as possible. "I know. And thank you for not arresting me. That would have been the nail in the coffin. How is the investigation going?"

"Why would he arrest you?" Geoffrey Wickers asked. "Is he militia? He doesn't look like militia. Where's his uniform?"

Wickers floated next to Mr Collingwood and inspected him, too.

I stared at Wickers, longing to tell them to get out of the way, but I would have looked like a complete idiot addressing thin air.

"The case is still ongoing and I can't talk about it," O'Malley combed his hair with his fingers. "But, no, at the moment I'm not going to arrest you for murder." There was that boyish smile again.

"Murder!" Lady Camilla goggled at us and her hand flew to her mouth. I tried not to laugh at the thought of a ghost worrying that I might be a murderer.

"That's a relief," I said. "Are you any closer to finding out who did it?"

O'Malley smiled boyishly, which made him look even more handsome. "We're closer than a Regency dance but not quite at a waltz." Then he added more seriously, "Like I said, I can't comment."

There was an awkward pause.

"Well, I'd better go," he said, standing up. "I've got a lot of interviews to do. I'll call you when we've finished with the tearoom. Thanks for your patience." He pronounced "thanks" as "tanks".

He walked into the hall and paused at the door. "Try not to let the whole situation get you down. We'll catch whoever did this." He pulled the door open and let himself out. I watched him walk down the street.

"He admires you," Lily said in my ear.

I jumped. "You shouldn't sneak up on people!"

Lily giggled. "Sorry."

"Well, young lady, why should you be accused of murder? What sort of woman are you?" Lady Camilla demanded, eyeing me suspiciously.

"I don't know why you're worried about murder," said Geoffrey Wickers, in a sarcastic tone. "You're already dead."

"So rude!" Lady Camilla huffed.

"I'm not a murderer. Someone was murdered in my tearoom yesterday, at the opening ceremony."

"You have a tearoom?" Lady Camilla asked.

"Yes. And I'm sorry if I'm not posh enough for you, but that's my job."

Mr Collingwood bowed. "Owning and operating a tearoom is a most respectable endeavour."

"Thank you," I said, sincerely. "I think so, too."

Lady Camilla softened a little. "I shall reserve judgement until I have seen the tearoom."

"I'm sure you'll love it," I responded.

I couldn't help smiling. Even if I were a murderer, these ghosts had nothing to fear from me.

CHAPTER 7

I took the ring off before going to bed, despite the ghosts' protests. "There's no way I'm sleeping with all of you floating around."

"We won't disturb you," Mr Collingwood said, in a reverent tone.

"But if you can see me even without the ring, and I'm asleep, I might as well take it off."

"She has a point," Mr Darby agreed.

I slept fitfully, waking up several times with the feeling that I was being watched. The ring sat on my bedside table but I didn't put it on, scared of seeing the ghosts at night. Was it Jane Austen's actual ring? Several times, I questioned my sanity and pondered what had happened. The last two days had been the strangest of my life.

The next morning, after lying in bed for a while, I sat up. I inspected the ring again, and my heart raced in anticipation as I put it on. I was ready and waiting for the ghosts to appear, but there was nothing. I expected one to float through the wall, but none did.

"I really am going mad," I said to myself.

"Who's going mad?" said a voice, and I jumped. It was Mr

Wickers, sitting next to me on the bed with his legs stretched out.

I yelped. "For goodness' sake! Can you all stop sneaking up on me?"

Mr Wickers gave a small bow. "My apologies, madam." He pointed to the ring. "If you press the stone, it will summon one of us."

"Really?"

"Indeed. Try it."

I pressed the ring, and sure enough, Mr Collingwood appeared out of thin air. I felt an increase in the familiar tingle in my body whenever the ghosts were near. "Your wish is my command, madam." He saw Mr Wickers. "Oh, you're here already."

"Just showing the new ring owner the ropes," Mr Wickers said, pointing to the ring.

Mr Collingwood made a small bow and simpered, then disappeared.

"So I'm not going mad, after all."

"I'm afraid not. We are ghosts, and we appear to you when you wear the ring. From what I saw, you didn't sleep very well."

I did a double-take. "You were watching me sleep?"

"Only briefly. You were moaning and groaning a lot."

I huffed and sat up. "Can you blame me?" I got out of bed. "I'm going to have a shower and get dressed. I expect you all to keep your eyes to yourselves and stay out of the bathroom."

Mr Wickers stood up, too. "I swear, on my word as a gentleman."

My eyes narrowed. "What about the others?"

"They will abide by the rules too. I can assure you. Besides, Mr Darby is too busy brooding to worry about anyone else."

I nodded. "He doesn't say much, does he? I get the

distinct feeling that he's judging me."

I looked hopefully at Mr Wickers, waiting for him to contradict me, but he just smiled.

I pressed the ring and Mr Collingwood appeared again. "Madam?"

"Get the others. We need to set some ground rules."

Mr Collingwood nodded, then disappeared and returned moments later with Lady Camilla, Mr Darby and Lily.

"If we're going to live together, there needs to be rules," I said. "No watching me sleep. In fact, stay out of my room when I go to bed, unless I'm awake. And when I'm in the bathroom, the toilet or getting dressed, stay away, then, too."

Mr Darby spoke in his deep voice. "Madam, I would never watch a lady when she is at her toilette."

"Good. Is that understood by everyone?" I looked at the others.

Everyone nodded except for Lady Camilla, who looked affronted. "I have no interest in seeing another lady in the bathroom. So vulgar."

"Excellent. I'm going to the bathroom, then coming back here to get dressed. See you all downstairs in the kitchen."

True to their word, the ghosts left me alone while I was in the bathroom and getting dressed. I went to the kitchen, made breakfast, then checked my messages. Other than a couple from friends, there was nothing.

I browsed social media and saw a new article from the local newspaper: "Local Businessman Stabbed in Tearoom Garden."

There were twenty-five comments beneath the post. I read the story, which was short and to the point: Larry Cunningham had been stabbed in the new Regency tearoom the day before, and the police were investigating.

The comments gave a variety of reactions. "RIP Larry," "Shocking," "Can't believe this happened in our town." No one mentioned me or the tearoom directly. That was good.

I thought about my own social media presence. I'd built my own website with basic details like the tearoom's location, opening hours and some photos I'd paid a local photographer to take. I also had profiles on various platforms and had spent the last few months posting teaser photos. Now, after all that build-up, I had egg on my face. I'd have to release a statement on social media, expressing sorrow and sending condolences to Larry's family. It was the right thing to do, and I could also mention that the tearoom would be closed for the time being.

"Another ring owner staring at a phone all the time," Lady Camilla said, scowling from behind my shoulder.

"Necessary evil, I'm afraid," I replied. "Who was the previous ring owner before me?"

"Young lady, you must visit the man's widow and pay your respects. That is the right thing to do. Never mind all this online nonsense." Lady Camilla waved a dismissive hand, ignoring my previous question.

"You know about the internet?"

"Of course we do. We haven't been asleep all these years. Remember, you're not the first ring owner, and you won't be the last."

I took a deep breath. "You're right. I need to visit Debbie. Here I am feeling sorry for myself, and she's lost her husband." And perhaps she might know who hated Larry so much that they killed him.

CHAPTER 8

Debbie lived in a block of flats in the western part of Sidmouth, famous for its Regency architecture. Uniform and elegant, built from honey-coloured stone and perched above street level with a sea view, the flats were snapped up at inflated prices whenever they came on the market.

I approached the entrance to the lobby and pressed the buzzer next to Debbie and Larry's nameplate.

"Hello?" said a voice.

"Hi, Debbie? It's me, Trinity Bishop. How are you? Can I come in?" I realised I should have brought flowers or at least a card. I could have kicked myself for the oversight.

"I suppose so," the speaker crackled.

The door buzzed and I pushed it open. Inside was a long, dark hall. A door at the end opened, and Debbie stood there, framed in light.

"Hello," I said in a sympathetic tone. "Thanks for letting me in."

Debbie led the way to the lounge, a large, high-ceilinged room with a bay window at the front of the flat. She gestured for me to sit on the large cream settee and took a seat opposite in a matching cream chair.

An awkward silence filled the room. Debbie looked pale and her eyes were red: she'd clearly been crying.

"I came because I wanted to give you my deepest condolences on your loss. I didn't get a chance yesterday."

Debbie looked at the floor. "Thank you. That's very kind."

Silence fell again, and I took a moment to look around the sparsely decorated room. The walls were magnolia, abstract art hung on three of the walls and a TV was in the far corner. Behind Debbie was a rustic pine cabinet holding glasses and vases. It looked as if it would be more at home in a cottage.

"Look, your husband and I didn't see eye to eye, but I am truly sorry. No one deserves to be murdered."

Debbie let out a sob, then pulled a tissue from her skirt pocket and wept into it.

I got up, sat on the armrest of her chair and put my arm round her. "It's a terrible situation, but the police will find out who did it and you'll get justice."

Then a thought struck me. In all the murder mystery TV shows I'd watched, the police officers always investigated the victim's partner first because nine times out of ten, they'd done it. But would Debbie be so upset if she had killed Larry? Maybe she was an excellent actress and it was all a show. As far as I knew, Debbie wasn't involved in the local amateur dramatic society, but I made a mental note to check.

Then I shook myself. It couldn't be Debbie. Stabbing Larry would have required power and strength. Debbie was thin and feeble-looking. What was I thinking? I came to visit her to give my sympathies, and here I was judging whether she'd killed her husband? I scolded myself for being so suspicious.

"Sorry." Debbie hiccupped after a while. "It's just such a terrible shock, and to be murdered with a knife in the back. It's horrible."

"It is," I agreed. "But why did Larry come to the tearoom?

He didn't want me to open the place at all, yet when I spoke to him yesterday, he said he wanted to see it for himself. Was that really why he came?"

Debbie nodded. "He was so silly and unbending about some things, and your tearoom was one of them. He thought there were enough cafés and such in the town already. I said to him, what's the harm in having one more? I liked the idea. It was refined and stood out from all the others."

"Thank you." That was nice of her. But the cheek of Larry, thinking he should decide what businesses there should be in the town!

"He wanted to put a damper on the opening and annoy you. It was stupid, I know. I said it would be better for him to stay away, but he wouldn't listen. And now look what's happened…" She started crying again. "If he hadn't gone, he wouldn't be dead."

A thought crossed my mind. The murderer might have killed Larry in my tearoom, but even if he or she hadn't come to the tearoom, the murderer would have found another place and time to kill him.

I waited a few moments before speaking. "I find it helpful to go over things that happen. You know, speak about it, to stop it swirling in my head."

Debbie dabbed at her nose with the tissue. "Really? Well, we arrived, went to the buffet, got a cup of tea and some food. Then we sat down at a table and you came over. A few other people came to speak to us afterwards. Then we went out to the garden, as he wanted to see that. And then David turned up."

"He's the man Larry had the argument with?"

"Yes. David stood in front of the table with a face like thunder." Debbie shook her head, trying to get rid of the thought.

"What did he say?"

"He said, 'Thought you'd seen the last of me?' Larry was

so angry and surprised to see him. We moved from Kent years ago, and we never expected to set eyes on David again."

"Why would David come all this way, then? There must have been a reason for him to turn up."

Debbie studied the floor. "I don't want to talk about it. It's all in the past: we put it behind us."

"Did you lose money? Was that it?"

Debbie shook her head.

I couldn't contain my next thoughts. "Do you think he murdered Larry? I mean, it's not a coincidence, is it? David turns up, and Larry is murdered a few minutes afterwards. If I were a detective, that's who I'd look into. Especially after their fight."

"David was spoiling for a fight, but Larry shouldn't have risen to it. It's so undignified at their age. But we both saw David leave. It can't have been him."

I nodded. "There's no way into the garden other than through the tearoom, and the garden wall is too high for someone to get over without a ladder. Did Larry come in for the opening ceremony? I don't remember seeing him when I was giving my speech."

Debbie sighed. "He said he'd rather watch paint dry and stayed in the garden."

A fatal mistake, I thought. "Did you see anyone outside with him? Or did you see anyone go into the garden?"

Debbie shook her head. "I wasn't the last to leave the garden; there were people behind me. And when I came inside, I had my back to the garden door."

"I probably had the best view, but I was so nervous that I didn't notice anything."

Debbie nodded. "Is your tearoom closed for now?"

"Yes. The forensics teams are going over it."

"I'm so sorry."

My eyebrows drew together slightly. "Are you apologising for someone killing your husband in my tearoom?"

That made Debbie giggle. "I suppose I am."

The mood lightened a little, and I was about to reply when the door buzzer sounded.

"I'd better get that," said Debbie, standing up. She left the room, and I heard her say, "Oh, hello, Officer. I'll buzz you in."

I stood up, then sat back down, not sure where to put myself. Why did I feel guilty? I hadn't murdered Larry, and I had every right to visit the widow of the murder victim.

I heard footsteps and DI O'Malley came in. "Hello," I said, trying to sound casual.

He frowned slightly. "Hello."

"Take a seat," said Debbie, behind him. He went to the chair where Debbie had been sitting and sat down.

An awkward silence fell. DI O'Malley met my eyes. "I've come to speak to Mrs Cunningham."

"Yes," I replied. Then the penny dropped. "Oh, so you want me to leave?"

"Nothing personal." He looked at me and I felt myself melt under his hypnotic gaze. "But I have to work my charm on someone else now."

I bit my lip. "Um, bye, then, Debbie. If you need anything, just ask." I got up and brushed some imaginary dirt from my tunic.

Debbie gave me a quick smile and showed me out, leaving me feeling rather foolish on the doorstep.

CHAPTER 9

On my way back, I decided to drop in at Aunt Ruby's house. My cousin Francis was sat at the kitchen table. Francis was twenty-eight and had only recently become a full-time police officer after a string of dead-end jobs. Aunt Ruby had hoped it would finally give him a purpose in life. So far, it seemed to have had a positive effect.

He'd always been gangly, and his police uniform didn't change that, even with a stab vest on top. Eight years younger than me, he'd been at primary school when I left Sidmouth for London with Dean, the man who would be my husband for the next twenty years.

"Are you on duty?" I asked, plonking myself down next to him.

"Taking a break," he said, through a mouthful of cake. "I've been told to stay clear of the murder case because we're related – before you ask."

"So you can't tell me what's happening with the investigation?"

Francis shook his head. "Sadly not. I'm being kept in the dark. Conflict of interest."

"Indeed," said Aunt Ruby as she came in. She went to the sink and turned on the taps, filling the washing-up bowl with water.

"So, give me the lowdown on DI O'Malley," I said.

Francis sat up straight and his eyes widened. "You fancy him, too?"

"You'd have to be blind not to find him attractive," I admitted.

Francis flung up his hands. "He's all the rage! He came from Belfast a couple of weeks ago to replace DI Hobbs, although he's originally from Dublin. He was working in Belfast Police when he met his wife, and now he's moved here to be near her, though now she's his ex-wife. She ran off to Exmouth with a woman, but he wanted to be near his kids, so he followed. Apparently it's all amicable – I don't see how." Francis paused only to draw breath. "All the women are raving over him. Even Teresa, and she's got a heart of stone."

"Really?" I went to the kitchen counter and helped myself to a slice of cake. I knew it was stress eating, but I didn't care. What I'd worked towards for the last six months had gone completely askew, and cake was the only remedy. "Does he live in Sidmouth?"

Francis shook his head. "He's renting a flat in Exmouth at the moment. Has the kids every other weekend."

"It's a shame they couldn't stay together for the kids. How old are they?"

"The boy is seven and the girl is nine."

"Young, then. No wonder he wants to be around as they grow up. What's he like to work with?"

"I've not worked with him yet; he's only been here a couple of weeks. Baptism by fire, though. A murder in his first month." Francis shook his head. "The station is buzzing with excitement. Normally, the most exciting thing that happens round here is a burglary."

"Francis!" Aunt Ruby admonished. "A man has been murdered and you think it's exciting?"

Francis shrugged. "It's true! I'm not saying a murder isn't bad."

As much as I wanted to talk about DI Handsome, aka O'Malley, there were more pressing things. There was no point beating around the bush with Francis. I just had to ask, "Are you sure they haven't told you anything about the case?"

"Nothing. It's all secret squirrel." Francis curled his hands up to imitate claws and stuck his bottom lip under his front teeth.

I laughed. "You always cheer me up. O'Malley said the CSI team would finish today."

"We haven't had a fatal stabbing in Sidmouth for decades, so I've no idea. I can't see how it can be much longer, though. The CSI team came from Exeter, and there's lots of things they need to do back there, so I'm sure it won't be long. Anyway, from what I heard, you were talking in front of thirty witnesses when the murder happened."

"I thought you weren't being told anything?"

"I'm not. I heard that in town."

"I bet everyone's gossiping about it."

"Of course they are!" Francis raised his eyebrows. "Nobody seems sad about his death, though, which won't help the investigation. So many wild theories are being aired about who did it and why."

"Like what?" I said, with my mouth full of cake.

Francis leaned forward. "Larry rubbed plenty of people up the wrong way. Gary from the barbershop at the top end of town had a heated debate with him a few weeks ago. Someone said Larry had refused to pay for a haircut."

"That's not a very wild theory," I said. "No one would kill for that small an amount."

"There's more, though. Apparently all the pot plants

round Gary's door were killed. Someone dumped salt in them. Gary accused Larry, but he denied it."

"So there was a feud?"

"Exactly. Another rumour is that Ruth Fielder held a seance with Larry, Debbie and some other people a few weeks ago, and Larry scoffed at it all. Then Ruth said she heard from someone on the 'other side' that Larry had done a terrible thing."

"What?"

"No one knows; the spirit didn't say. Anyway, she reckons a spirit took possession of someone's body and killed Larry as retribution."

I sighed. "At least the theories don't involve me."

Francis blinked and said nothing.

"Please tell me no one's saying I did it."

"There's the odd comment about you. People wondering whether you had a motive."

For a moment, I closed my eyes and wished I was back in London and not living in a small Devon town where everyone knew everyone else. I decided not to enquire further. "There must be some evidence, though. Weren't there fingerprints on the knife?"

"Wiped clean."

"Or they used a cloth or gloves when they murdered him," Aunt Ruby said, from the sink.

Francis's police radio crackled. "Control to all available units. We have a ten fifty-four at the Byes. Please respond. Over."

Francis sighed, then pressed the button on his radio and spoke into it. "Control, this is Delta Echo One. Copy that, I'm en route to the Byes. Over."

"What's happened?" I asked.

"The sheep have escaped again. They're such a nuisance: right bunch of Houdinis."

CHAPTER 10

Back home, I put the ring on and updated the ghosts.

"Paying your respects to the widow was the right thing to do," Lady Camilla said, approvingly.

Mr Collingwood nodded to Lady Camilla. "You were right to instruct the young lady. You're so knowledgeable and wise."

Lily rolled her eyes. "When will you take us out? I want to see Sidmouth again. It's boring being stuck here."

"Again?" I said, raising my eyebrows.

"We're not supposed to talk about previous ring-holders," Lady Camilla snapped.

"So you've been to Sidmouth before." I put my hand on my hip.

"Of course we've been here," Lady Camilla huffed. "Jane Austen brought us here in the summer of 1801."

My eyes widened. "Tell me everything about it."

Lily giggled. "Jane fell in love."

"Yes, I heard that. With a clergyman who died shortly after." I remembered reading about it in one of the many biographies about her, thrilled that she'd visited my home-town during her lifetime.

Mr Collingwood straightened himself. "She was consumed with grief."

Lady Camilla interrupted him. "She was indeed very sad, but given time, she got over it."

I nodded sympathetically, and I wanted to know more about Jane Austen's time in Sidmouth.

"When can we go out?" Lily asked.

"How far can you go from the ring when I have it on?"

Lily pouted. "Only about a hundred and fifty feet. We've visited your neighbours on both sides. They're out most of the day, though, and when they come home, all they do is watch TV. It's so boring. I want to get out and about. It's been over two hundred years."

"So you weren't in Sidmouth with the previous ring-holder, then?" I asked slyly.

Mr Wickers wagged a finger at me. "Ah-ah-ah. No, you don't. You're not getting any information from us about previous ring-holders."

"I think it's a stupid rule. I mean, what happens if you tell me? Do they die? Do I die? Does the sky cave in?" I pointed to the ceiling.

Lady Camilla stepped forward. "It's our rule now. Two of our ring-holders contacted each other once, and, well, it wasn't pretty. It's better that you know nothing."

I narrowed my eyes. "What if I don't want to be a ring-holder any more? What happens then?"

Mr Darby floated to the front. "Why would you not wish to be a ring-holder, pray?"

"I'd like a bit of peace and quiet, for a start. Why do I even have the ring in the first place?"

Mr Wickers turned to Lily with an exasperated look. "She has just opened a Jane Austen-themed tearoom, and she wonders why she was given the ring."

That was interesting. Perhaps you had to be a Jane Austen fanatic to have the ring. That made sense, but there were plenty of us in the world. There must have been something else about me, too.

I sighed. "All right, I can see I won't get anywhere today. But I won't stop asking or trying to find out more." I turned to Lily. "I'll wear the ring next time I go out."

"Yippee!" Lily did a backflip in the air. "We can help you find out who murdered the man in the tearoom."

I thought for a moment. "Actually, that's not a bad idea. One thing is strange, though. I thought the police would arrest David, the man Larry argued with at my tearoom opening. They must have questioned him, at least."

"Undoubtedly," said Mr Darby.

"Even though Debbie and every other guest saw David leave before Larry's murder, I want to speak to him myself. First, I need to find out where he's staying."

"Can you use that thing?" Mr Darby pointed to my laptop, sat on the table.

So the ghosts know about computers. Their last ring-holder must have been modern. "Not for that. I'll ask Aunt Ruby. She knows most of the B&B owners in the town."

I took out my phone and composed a message. Not long after, I got the reply I was after: David was staying at the Pebbles B&B. Owned by Meg, a friend of Aunt Ruby's, it was one of the cheaper B&Bs away from the seafront. Although I hadn't been inside, I'd driven past many times. It was a large detached house with a welcoming frontage decorated with baskets of flowers.

I grabbed my bag and jacket, and put on my shoes. "Don't forget to keep the ring on," said Lily, floating round the house after me. "I can't wait to get out and about."

I felt some anxiety about what might happen, but a promise was a promise. "Well, the B&B isn't far, so don't get too excited."

The ghosts followed me from my house to the B&B, commenting on Sidmouth.

"Seems like a pleasant town still," Mr Wickers said.

"Do they really need so many barbers?" asked Mr Collingwood.

"You can never have too many barbers," Mr Darby replied. "A gentleman should always look presentable, but not fall into vanity."

"A bookshop! How delightful!" exclaimed Lady Camilla. "You must go in so that I can have a look." Then she sniffed at a woman in a multicoloured dress. "Such bold colours."

Mr Wickers pointed out two workmen with oily coveralls, eating sandwiches on a bench. "At least she is clean. You would scarcely know these as gentlemen in such attire."

I jumped as a sports car roared by, bass thumping. Mr Darby shook his head disdainfully. "What need has a man for such loud contraptions? Do they seek to impress with noise where appearances fail?"

"Didn't you have a fancy carriage when you were alive?" I asked him.

His face clouded over. "I had several carriages, but I was not so vulgar as to make myself stand out."

As we continued down the high street, Lady Camilla spied two women in the window of a café, chatting. "Now *there* is civility."

"Wait until you see my tearoom. I think you will approve."

We reached the B&B and I rang the bell. Meg opened the door.

"Hello, Meg, I'm Ruby's niece, Trinity."

"Hello, dear. Ruby texted me earlier and said to expect you. You're after talking to David?"

"I am. Is that okay?"

"It is with me, dear, but he might not be so keen. Come in. He's in room seven. I wouldn't normally say who's staying here, but there was a murder. Up the stairs, turn left, keep going until you get to the end. The number's on the door."

I thanked Meg and followed her directions until I found myself outside David's door. I knocked hard and loud, and about ten seconds later, the door opened.

It took David a moment to realise I wasn't Meg, then another to recognise me. "Can I help?" His expression was as bland as a blank page.

My ghostly entourage, who'd trailed upstairs after me, vanished through the wall into David's room.

"Do you remember me? I own the tearoom. Trinity Bishop."

"Yes, I remember."

"Can we talk?"

"I have nothing to say."

"Not even to apologise for that row at my opening event?" That wasn't how I'd planned to take the conversation forward, but David had annoyed me.

He seemed to weigh my words, then shook his head. "I'm sorry the row happened in your tearoom, but I don't regret it. And I'm not sorry that man is dead."

My mouth fell open in disbelief. "What?"

"Look, I've got nothing to say to you. I've told the police everything I need to. Sorry, but not sorry." And with that, he closed the door in my face.

I stood staring at the door, blinking in disbelief.

Well, that told me. He clearly wasn't going to speak to be civil. I walked away, then realised all the ghosts were in his room.

"Hey!" I whispered. "What are you doing in there?"

Mr Wickers' face appeared through the wall. "Just having a nose around for you. It's not a bad room, actually. Nicely decorated, with a large double bed. He's sitting on the bed looking into space. I'd warrant he's thinking about how rude he was to you. Shocking language to use with a lady, I must say. A gentleman should never brush off a lady so directly."

"How long will you be?"

"Hold on." Mr Wickers disappeared for a moment, then came back. "Lily is checking the wardrobe and Mr Darby, the suitcase. Then we can depart."

He disappeared again, and I stood awkwardly outside the door.

They all reappeared a minute later. "You may go," Lady Camilla instructed.

"Find anything interesting?" I asked, as we walked down the street.

"Nothing to help with your investigation," Mr Darby replied. "He appears dull and boring."

"No secret written confession, then?"

"Sadly, no."

I stopped walking and looked at the turquoise ring on my finger. "This is the real Jane Austen ring?"

"Yes!" Lily said excitedly. "She was given it in 1796 and had it until she died."

"And we got on so well that she immortalised us in her most famous novel," Lady Camilla said proudly. "Changing our names slightly, of course."

My phone rang. I looked at the display: DI O'Malley. I answered straight away, a lump of guilt in my throat. Had David called him?

"Hello." I tried to sound casual.

"DI O'Malley," he said, in a matter-of-fact tone. "Trinity, we've finished at your tearoom. You can reopen whenever you like."

"Really?" I tried not to squeal.

"Yes, really."

"That's great news. Thanks."

"Take care now and keep the customers alive, okay?"

I giggled. "I'll try."

The call ended and I turned to the ghosts. "Did you hear that? The tearoom can reopen!"

CHAPTER 11

I sighed and made a mental list of what needed doing. One of my famous to-do lists was definitely in order. In the meantime, I phoned Carol and Emma to let them know they would be needed the next day for the tearoom's reopening.

When I went inside the tearoom, the ghosts inspected it. Lily flew about excitedly, Mr Darby floated around with a critical eye and Mr Collingwood followed behind Lady Camilla as she took it all in.

"It is satisfactory," she said, eventually, looking around her.

"I'm glad you approve," I responded as I finished off my to-do list. I wasn't sure I actually was glad, but it was all I could think to say.

It took me most of the day to get the tearoom into a fit state for customers. The dirty crockery and crumbs of food from two days before were still there, and there was finger-print powder to clean up, too. Then I prepared Devon apple cakes and scones under the watchful eyes of five ghosts.

The next day, at exactly ten o'clock, everything was ready.

Under Lady Camilla's direction, I'd done my hair in an authentic style, drawing it into a knot at the nape and curling the tendrils that fell loosely around my face. Lady Camilla nodded her approval.

"Are we good to go?" Carol asked, looking at her watch. "Do I look all right?"

Carol was also dressed in Regency costume. That was one reason why she'd taken the job. That, and her in-depth knowledge of Jane Austen's novels. We'd talked for hours about them when I interviewed her.

"You look fantastic. I love the white cap. Are you Mrs Bennet today?"

"Definitely." Carol put the back of her hand on her forehead, feigning agitation. "My poor nerves…"

I chuckled. "Emma, I need you in the kitchen today, if that's all right?"

Emma nodded and walked into the kitchen.

"She's a quiet one!" Mr Wickers said, watching her go.

Lady Camilla tutted. "Always an eye for the young ladies."

It took an agonising half hour for the first customers to come in: a group of ladies in their seventies who ordered tea and scones. I served them myself, and fussed over them until more customers arrived.

By lunchtime, the tearoom was filling up. Mr Darby brooded in the tea garden, while Mr Collingwood stayed close to Lady Camilla.

"Ooh, this is delightful," said Lily, clasping her hands. "All these people in your tearoom. How exciting!" She swished to the window and looked out. "It's stopped raining. That might bring more people to the town."

There was a lull at about two o'clock, so I fled to the kitchen for a brief break. I grabbed a scone and smothered it with cream and jam. It tasted divine.

The kitchen was still clean and tidy, thanks to Emma, but

she looked tired and flustered. "Why don't you have a break?" I said. "I can manage here."

"Thanks." Emma took out her packed lunch and helped herself to a cold drink, then disappeared into the small area next to the kitchen that was the staffroom.

A table of four ordered my signature Highbury High Tea, a nod to the book *Emma*. I'd spent hours working on it and the menu ran as follows:

Hartfield Ham Sandwiches: Delicate slices of ham on buttered white bread, crusts removed
Box Hill Cucumber Bites: Fresh cucumber slices served in buttered brown bread, crusts removed
Miss Bates's Devilled Eggs
Mr Knightley's Fruit Scones: Traditional scones served with clotted cream and strawberry jam
Jane Fairfax's Lemon Cakes: Little lemon-flavoured sponge cakes
The Westons' Walnut Biscuits: Crunchy biscuits containing walnuts.

I was busy placing cakes and finger sandwiches on the stand when Lady Camilla drifted in. "Can't your maid do that?"

I paused. "If you mean Emma, she's taking a break."

Lady Camilla sniffed. "I suppose at least you have servants, even if you don't manage them very well."

"Emma isn't my servant. She works in my tearoom."

"Serving meals. Do you pay her?"

"Yes, of course."

"She is a servant, then," Lady Camilla said smugly. "I think I shall like it here with you. You're much nicer and certainly more interesting than the last ring-owner."

"Who was the last ring-owner?"

Mr Wickers suddenly appeared and stepped forwards, a

glint in his eye. "Are you trying to find out about the other ring-owners again?"

"Yes."

He came closer and whispered in my ear, "If you're nice to me, I might tell you."

"I'm always nice to you," I said, affronted.

"I know you are," said a voice in the doorway, and I jumped. It was my best friend, Holly.

"Sorry, I was, um…" I shot Mr Wickers a warning look.

"I just came to check everything's okay on your first day. I'd have come sooner, but it's been nonstop. It's nearly Beltane and the shop's stupidly busy."

"That's good." I kept my focus on filling the three-tiered stand with food.

"How's the investigation going?"

I looked up. "If you mean how are the local police dealing with the crime, I have no idea. I suppose I should be grateful they haven't arrested me."

"Isn't Francis sorting that out?"

"No chance. They're keeping him out of it. Conflict of interest, you see. Probably for the best, really."

"You were always good at figuring things out, Trinity. Every time we've done escape rooms, you've always been the one to crack the clues."

"That's hardly the same as a murder investigation."

"It's all puzzles, though, and you were always good at them. Even in school."

I couldn't help smiling as I recalled the good old days of school with Holly. I'd loved it and had never wanted it to end. I wept when we finished our A-levels. But a few months later, I met Dean when he came to Sidmouth on holiday with his family, then ran off to London to be near him. School had been long forgotten.

I dragged myself back to the present. "I do want to try and figure out what happened. I can't move on until the murderer is caught. I mean, what if they try it again? Maybe it's a mad serial killer."

"I hadn't thought of that," Holly said.

Carol poked her head round the door. "We have a problem out front."

CHAPTER 12

"What?" I asked, full of dread.

Carol pointed to the tearoom. "A couple of weirdos want to see where Larry was murdered. I've told them they have to order something or go, so they're looking at the menu. Thing is, it looks like they're filming in here."

I sighed. "I'll take out this order and see them off." I picked up the cake stand and headed out.

The couple in question were sitting at a window table. They were in their thirties, dressed in scruffy jeans and T-shirts. I delivered the Highbury High Tea, then went over and pulled out my notepad. On their table sat a video camera with a tiny red light on. They were definitely recording.

"I'm sorry, but we don't allow video recording in the tearoom," I said, making my voice as flat as possible.

The man looked up at me. "We wondered where the man was murdered."

"What?"

"The man in the paper who was murdered here," said the woman. "Where did it happen?"

I frowned. "Are you only here to visit the scene of a murder?"

"Er, no. I mean, yes and no. We're digital broadcasters."

"You're what?"

"You know, vloggers. We visit the scene of a murder to see if we can sense the ghost."

"Ooh, ghost hunters!" cried Lily, peeping round me. "They are my most favourite to tease."

"Tease?" As soon as I said it, I wished I hadn't.

Both their brows furrowed and I braced myself. "No, we prefer coffee to tea," the man said.

Thankful for the misunderstanding, I tapped my order pad with the pen. "This is a tearoom. Please either order something or leave. Besides, there's no such thing as ghosts." I looked at Lily floating above the table, who giggled.

The couple smiled at me. "Everyone says that, but we've seen a few."

"Ask them who," said Mr Collingwood. "I might have met them."

I glanced at him, then back at the couple. "What sort of ghosts do you think you've met?"

"We went on one of those nights where you camp in a haunted house," said the woman, enthusiastically. "It was terrifying. I heard a ghost: a man from the fourteen hundreds, who was hung for theft."

"And I saw a ghostly figure one night when it was dusk, just outside Shepton Mallet," the man added.

A few days ago, I would have thought them mad. Then I looked at Lily and Mr Collingwood and realised that maybe I was the mad one.

The tearoom doorbell tinkled. A party of five were hovering by the counter.

"I'll be with you in one moment," I told them, and turned back to the couple. "As I said, if you want to ghost-hunt here, then you need to purchase something. And switch off that camera."

The man rolled his eyes."In that case, tea and scones for two, please." He stopped the recording, grumbling, and I went to look after the new arrivals.

Once I was safely back in the kitchen, I let out the huff I'd been holding in. Then I peeked out and saw that Lily and Mr Collingwood had sat down at the couple's table. Lily was waving a hand in front of the man's face to try and get his attention. I shook my head and chuckled.

When I delivered their tea and scones, Mr Collingwood got up. "Typical ghost hunters. Utterly clueless." I just managed to stop myself from saying anything.

I took the new arrivals' order and went back to the kitchen, followed by Lily. "It has to be deep magic for anyone to see or hear a ghost," she said, pointing to the turquoise ring on my finger.

"Deep magic made this ring? Is that what you mean? What exactly is deep magic? Is there shallow magic?"

"Sort of—"

Holly came in again through the kitchen door that led outside. "Nice to see the place busy." She walked straight through Lily, who sighed and floated to the other side of the room.

I stared at her for a moment, speechless. "Er, yes, thank you."

"By the way, before I go, I have gossip about the murder." Holly picked up a scone. "Are these fresh?"

"Of course they are. What have you heard?"

Holly took a bite. "Larry and the SBC secretary, Heather, hated each other."

"I knew that. And?"

"And she was at the opening. She could have murdered him."

"Just because they hated each other doesn't mean she

killed him. There seems to be a long list of people who hated Larry. Maybe they all did it!"

"All I'm saying is that it's worth looking into."

"I shouldn't be looking into it, though. That's for the police."

Mr Darby swept in and examined Holly as she chewed. "She's right, you know. It is worth looking into."

I sighed. "All right, I'll talk to her. It won't do any harm."

Holly looked pleased I'd changed my mind, and I couldn't help feeling I was doing the legwork for her.

"She's a notorious workaholic and stays late most nights."

"She's an estate agent, isn't she? At Hardy Estates?" I asked.

"That's it."

"As soon as the tearoom's shut, I'll drop in and talk to her. See what she remembers."

CHAPTER 13

That evening, as I was locking the door behind Emma and Carol, I turned and saw Mr Collingwood pointing to the bookstand. I was surprised that he was alone; he was usually simpering next to Lady Camilla. In my view, Jane Austen had captured them both perfectly in *Pride and Prejudice*, though I didn't say that out loud. I made a mental note to ask the ghosts what they thought of their characterisations in the book. If I'd been Mr Collingwood, I'd have been annoyed that I was portrayed as a simpering, undesirable, creepy cousin. No one would want to be remembered like that.

I went over to him. "Hello, Mr Collingwood. How are you this afternoon?"

Mr Collingwood made a small bow. "Pardon me, madam. I was perusing your book collection, and I could not help noticing the book *Sidmouth: A History of Smuggling*. So I read it.

"Oh yes! That's on my to-read pile." I walked over and picked up a copy. It was a thin book, written by a local author. I leafed through it, looking at the pictures of Sidmouth and the English Channel in the past. Then I read the blurb on the back:

Step into the shadowy corners of Sidmouth's past, where law and order were often elusive concepts, and smuggling was a clandestine game that tempted men and women alike. Sidmouth: A History of Smuggling *pulls back the curtain on this quaint seaside town's not-so-innocent history – from the devious tactics employed by smugglers to the valiant efforts of the local law enforcement. Illustrated with archival photos and detailed maps, this book reveals the hidden tunnels, secret coves, and intricate networks that made Sidmouth a smuggler's paradise. A must-read for history buffs and lovers of local lore, this book is as informative as it is thrilling. Discover Sidmouth's dark past and gain a new appreciation for this seemingly tranquil locale. You'll never look at its scenic coastline the same way again.*

"You know, I grew up here, but I never once bothered to read up on the local history of smuggling," I said. "Apparently, it was rife. Everyone was involved, because they smuggled tea, brandy and tobacco. Most people couldn't afford them because of the high taxes."

"Indeed, madam. When the esteemed Miss Austen visited the town with us in 1801, there was much talk of the smuggling that took place, although none of us saw any of it. I believe that, as you say, everyone was involved."

I decided not to point out that Mr Collingwood was telling me about a past ring-wearer, which went directly against the ghosts' self-imposed rule. In addition, I was also eager to hear as much as possible about Jane Austen.

"If you turn to page fifty-six of the book, you will see a passage that mentions a missing treasure map." I did as Mr Collingwood asked and turned to the correct page, then read it aloud.

"The Lost Map of Sidmouth's Smugglers.

"One of the most enduring smuggling legends to come out of Sidmouth is the tale of the lost treasure map. Said to be created by Thomas 'Black-Eye' Elmore, a notorious smuggler who led one of the most well-organised smuggling rings in the early eighteen hundreds, the map was said to outline the locations of his hidden gold, silver and other valuable goods.

"Black-Eye Elmore and his crew were known for their cunningness and audacity, always eluding capture by the local authorities and the Royal Navy. They amassed a considerable fortune, most of which was never recovered. According to local legend, Elmore created a detailed map, showing where his treasure was hidden. However, he died in 1797 of scurvy and the map was lost forever.

"Over the years, many have claimed to be close to discovering the fabled map, but it remains lost to this day.

"Some consider it a myth, yet the truth remains: a considerable amount of treasure went missing, and the activities of Black-Eye Elmore and his crew are well-documented. Could it be that the map still awaits discovery, its secrets to be unravelled by one deemed worthy? Only time will tell."

When I finished reading, I looked up at Mr Collingwood, who gave me an appreciative nod. "That's an interesting passage," I said. "A hidden treasure map."

He gave a small bow. "When my good self and the other ghosts visited the town of Sidmouth in the year of our Lord 1801, with Miss Jane Austen, we, too, heard rumours of a treasure map. We found some clues to its whereabouts, but we were not fortunate enough to find the map itself."

"Wait a minute," I said, with a laugh. "Are you telling me there's a real treasure map hidden in the town?"

"Yes, ma'am."

I pursed my lips. Life was getting stranger and stranger by the day. "So where do you think the map is hidden?"

"We believe it was hidden in one of two public houses in the town: the Swan Inn or the Volunteer Inn."

"Both those pubs are still here. Did you go in them back then, with Jane Austen?"

Mr Collingwood gave me an awkward smile. "In Regency England, gentlewomen of good character did not frequent public houses – and especially not ladies of the middle and upper classes. It was considered improper, and inappropriate."

"So Jane Austen looked for the map but didn't find it, because it was probably hidden in a pub that she couldn't enter?"

Mr Collingwood bowed again.

I narrowed my eyes. "Why do I get the feeling that you want me to find the treasure map?"

"We would not presume, madam. However, finding the treasure would give you untold wealth."

A vision of a treasure map just like those in pirate movies crossed my mind: a parchment with a giant X showing where to dig. I didn't need lots of money, and there was no way I could visit a remote island to find hidden treasure – assuming it hadn't already been found or if it was even on an island. But then I remembered something my ex-husband had said to me not long before we split up. *You're just not adventurous any more.* That had stung.

Mr Collingwood coughed, rousing me from my thoughts. "Sorry, was there something else?" I asked.

"We believe there may be an object amongst the hidden treasure which would help us reach the afterlife."

My eyebrows shot up. "Really?"

He nodded.

"Do you know what the item is?"

"We are not certain, but we believe it may be related to the turquoise ring on your finger. Possibly it was forged by the same jeweller. Previous ring-holders have learnt that other works by that jeweller were stolen by Black-Eye Elmore. If you find the treasure, that may hold the key to our glorious ascension."

"Okay, so if I find the map and then the treasure, I might actually be able to help you get to heaven?"

"Indeed."

"All right, I'm in." How could I not help? Only someone heartless would refuse.

Mr Collingwood looked around. "In? In where?"

"I mean, I'll do it."

Mr Collingwood smiled and bowed. "We will remain forever grateful to you, madam."

"Yes, well, I haven't found it yet."

CHAPTER 14

Holly had been right. Heather Hardy's estate agency officially closed at five, but when I finally said goodbye to the last customer, locked up and made my way across town to Hardy Estates, I could still see Heather inside and it was gone six. I remembered Heather being at the opening, but I couldn't recall seeing her in the tea garden, or in the tearoom while I had been giving my speech.

"We're closed," Heather mouthed, and pointed to the sign hanging on the door.

I opened the letterbox. "I just wanted to speak to you," I shouted through it. "About…" I was just about to say *the murder* when a couple walked by. "About Larry."

A moment later, Heather came over and unlocked the door. "Come in." She looked me up and down, probably because I was in jeans and a shirt rather than my Empire-line Regency dress. "Take a seat."

I went in, the five ghosts trailing behind me.

The office was big and minimalist. There were three separate desks, with Heather's at the front. Pristine photographs of upscale properties dangled from sleek wire hangers on plain white walls. The streamlined furniture and organised desks gave it an air of professionalism.

Heather was dressed in a smart black shift-dress with a white blouse underneath. Her hair was perfect and her make-up so smooth that it looked as though a professional had applied it. I envied women like her with the time and skill to apply make-up so well. It was a skill I'd never mastered.

Heather indicated a chair in front of her desk and I sat down. Her computer screen faced her, but I could see it a little. It showed a website: *Vegas Poker 2U*. Then she touched the side of the screen and it went blank.

The ghosts floated about, inspecting the office and commenting on the décor.

"How can I help you, Trinity?" Heather smiled, but it was a *I don't really want you here* kind of smile. It was very different from her friendly, open behaviour at the opening, and I hadn't expected it.

I also hadn't thought about what to say once I was in Heather's office. "Oh, er, I suppose you've heard that I'm a suspect in Larry's murder." That was a half-truth. Everyone was a suspect, including me.

Heather's eyebrows rose. "Really?"

"I know. Because he opposed my tearoom, they think I might have stabbed him during the opening ceremony."

"That's ridiculous. Why would you kill him when the place had just opened?"

That was the start I needed. "Exactly. Did the police interview you, too?"

"They came here wanting to know what Larry did at the Sidmouth Business Consortium. I'm secretary there, have been for years."

"What was he like when he was doing consortium business?" I remembered the gruff, antagonistic man who'd spoken against my tearoom. Maybe he was only like that with me.

"He was horrible to everyone."

"Including you?"

"Including me."

Mr Darby paused by some photographs of a property. "This house is an excellent investment."

Lady Camilla joined him and inspected the photo. "The main entrance is far too small. I don't like it."

I shook myself. "Um, that must have made things awkward."

"I couldn't stand him. When he was voted in as chairman, I nearly resigned. I only stayed because I'd built up the consortium from scratch, and I wasn't going to let him ruin it."

Mr Wickers floated down and examined Heather's face. "She's lying about something."

"Takes one to know one," Mr Darby responded.

I was dying to say something but stopped myself. If the ghosts wanted to follow me everywhere, I would have to learn to hold my tongue when other people were around. Or end up being known as an eccentric who talked to herself all the time.

"Was there anything in particular that made you dislike him?"

Heather snorted. "He treated me like everyone else – with disdain and nastiness. His wife's upset now, but I'm sure that in a few weeks she'll realise she's better off without him."

Mr Wickers sniggered. "Nasty. I like it."

"How did you work together?" I continued.

"We didn't. Well, he'd bark commands at me, and I'd do the bare minimum to communicate with him. Whenever he came into the consortium meetings, I'd sit as far away as possible and ignore him." Heather gave me a satisfied smile.

"Wow. You must really have hated him."

Heather's eyes narrowed. "Not enough to kill him, if that's what you mean."

I gave a small laugh. "Oh no, of course not."

"I never went out to your tea garden, mainly because Larry was there. It's strange, though. He told everyone he wasn't coming, so what he was doing there is anyone's guess."

"It surprised me that he turned up too," I said. "He told me he wanted to see it for himself."

Heather harrumphed. "He was only there to stir up trouble. There'd be no other reason for him to turn up, not even to spite you because he wasn't invited."

"Oh, but I did invite him. I hoped we could bury the hatchet, and that once he saw the tearoom in all its glory he would change his mind."

Heather shook her head. "I admire your optimism, but once that horrid man had an opinion about something, he never changed it."

"Did he upset many people?"

"Of course. He loved being chairman of the consortium, and he used it to his full advantage."

"How did he get voted in as chairman, though? Surely the other members must have liked him enough to vote for him?"

Heather looked scornful. "Ha! It's a poisoned chalice. No one wants the job."

"Really?"

"Absolutely. There's no pay and you have to go to endless meetings. You don't actually have any power."

"There must be some perks of the job, though. Otherwise Larry wouldn't have taken it."

"He liked to feel important, Trinity. He liked labels and titles. Being chairman added to that." Heather swung herself back and forth in her swivel chair, then leaned forward. "You know, when you were looking for premises for your tearoom, you should have come to me."

She was clearly fishing for an apology, but I wouldn't bite. "A friend of a friend told me about the tearoom premises, and

I knew it would be just right, so I jumped on it. I'll know where to come next time, though. If the tearoom is as successful as I hope, I'll be looking for a larger space."

Heather sat back. "Well, I'll be here whenever you need me."

I stood up. "Did you like the tearoom?"

"It was enchanting; the tourists will love it. I haven't read any of Jane Austen's novels, but I love the adaptations. That *Pride and Prejudice* one with Keira Knightley is my favourite."

Hmm, I thought. *Most diehard fans prefer the one with Colin Firth.* "Never read one of her books? Tut tut," said Lady Camilla, from the other side of the office. "And Keira Knightley was a very contentious choice."

"I can recommend the books. I've read them all many times over."

"Which is your favourite?" Mr Darby asked. He was floating just beside Heather's left shoulder.

"Which is your favourite?" Heather asked, almost at the same time.

"*Pride and Prejudice,*" I told them.

"I must get round to reading it."

"I have copies for sale in the tearoom. Special editions on smooth glossy paper, with a delightful cover."

"I'll pop in and buy one next time I'm passing." She sat up. "If that's all, I need to get on. Such a lot of emails to answer."

"Oh, um, thanks." Even though I hadn't planned what I was going to ask, I felt as though I had unfinished business with Heather.

"Look, if you want to know more about what Larry was like, you'd be better off talking to Susan Mason. She's one of the consortium's trustees."

"Was she close to Larry?"

Heather sniggered. "Oh yes. Very, very close."

"Estate agents' offices are so dull," Lily whined as we returned to the tearoom. "I thought I would die of boredom."

I laughed. "You're already dead."

"It depends on the property for sale," said Lady Camilla. "Most of those were merely small houses for ordinary people."

"Small?" I stopped. "One of them was on sale for two million pounds."

"Two million pounds!" Lady Camilla gave me an amused look. "In today's money, that's a trifle. Back in my day, though, only the king had that sort of money."

"Inflation is a strange thing," said Mr Darby.

The ghosts continued talking. I tuned them out and thought about my conversation with Heather. I hadn't learned much about either Heather or Larry. Heather seemed to be a self-assured, no-nonsense businesswoman; however, I only had her word for it that she hadn't entered the garden and spoken to Larry. I really shouldn't have gone to speak to her and felt a little ashamed that I'd been persuaded to go. But at the same time, my curiosity was getting the better of me and I wanted to talk to Susan. I'd decide in the morning if I should go and see her.

As soon as I was home, a wave of tiredness came over me. I wanted to visit Susan Mason, as Heather had suggested, but it would have to wait.

CHAPTER 15

The next morning, at eight thirty, I knocked on Susan's front door. Her house sat on the outskirts of the town. Built in the nineteen thirties, it had a large front garden, with bedding plants surrounding an immaculate lawn. At the side of the house, a gravel drive led to a garage.

I knew it was unusual to call on someone you hardly knew, at eight thirty in the morning, but with the tearoom opening at ten, I couldn't pick and choose my time. Yes, I was starting to get obsessed, but the murder, however awful, was ruining my dream of the perfect tearoom. I had to take action. That was what I was telling myself anyway.

I'd left the magical ring at home for once, wanting some time alone.

Susan opened her door and she recognised me immediately. She was in her late forties, average height for a woman, but I towered above her. She wore black trousers and a floral top. "Hello, Trinity, what can I do for you?"

"I've brought you some treats from my tearoom. Can I come in? I won't be long."

Susan looked at the cardboard cake box I held. "How lovely. Yes, of course, do come in."

I followed her inside. The house was small, opening directly onto the lounge. Beyond, I could see a small kitchen.

"Do sit down." Susan indicated the sofa. I was about to sit when I remembered the cakes and scones and handed over the box.

Susan peeked inside. "Yummy. I shouldn't really, but I deserve a treat."

"Oh, has something bad happened?"

She shrugged. "Just, you know, all this business with Larry."

I nodded. "It's a terrible shock for everyone."

"That dashing Irish detective was here yesterday. He said he wanted to confirm a few things from the day of the murder."

"Confirm things?" I wondered what needed confirming.

"Yes. You know, where I was sitting, whether I talked to Larry that day. That sort of thing." That was strange. Why would O'Malley single Susan out?

"I think he's visiting most of the guests who came to the opening." I wasn't sure that was true, even though I said it.

She snorted. "That'll take him a while; there were lots of people there. It was a lovely event. Except for the murder, of course. That goes without saying."

"It doesn't sound like they're any closer to finding the culprit," I mused. "I suppose they're doing their best."

"Isn't your cousin a policeman?"

"Yes, but they won't tell Francis anything, because of me. It's very annoying."

"I heard you were a suspect." Was there a hint of spite in her voice?

"Everyone who was at the opening is a suspect."

Susan nodded. "I suppose they have to eliminate every-one, which is what they were doing with me."

"So, did you know Larry very well?" I asked.

"Well… We used to get on like a house on fire."

I sensed Susan was keeping something back. "But not lately?"

Her eyes narrowed. "No, not lately. But as I told that handsome detective, that wasn't enough to kill him. It was just—" She closed her mouth.

"Just…?"

"Nothing. It was over nothing. You know how silly arguments can be."

"Heather said the consortium members didn't like him. So it wasn't the same for you?"

"Oh, he was abrasive. And sometimes a downright bully, but I never let him bully me. He liked it when people stood up to him. His wife, Debbie, is a complete wet blanket. Nice, of course, but she would let him get away with anything. So he did."

I remembered my visit to Debbie. She'd been quiet, but I'd put that down to her losing her husband.

"I heard Larry had an altercation with a man in the garden," Susan remarked. "I'm surprised they haven't arrested him."

"He left the tearoom before Larry was murdered."

"The perfect alibi, then." Susan smiled. "Too perfect. If I was in the police, that would be the first thing I'd check out."

"Did you socialise with Larry much?"

"Gosh, what a lot of questions!" Susan leaned forward. "One might almost think you'd come to investigate me, like the police. You've come all this way out of town early in the morning to speak to me."

I managed a nervous laugh. "I'm just a nosy tearoom owner, that's all. Although, I'd love to know why some heartless person murdered Larry on my opening day. It's been most inconvenient."

"Yes, very sad for you. Not what you were expecting at

all. Well, not what any of us were expecting. Least of all Larry." Susan stood up. "Well, don't let me keep you. You must have a thousand things to do now that the tearoom is properly open. Thank you so much for the cakes."

"Er, yes." I stood up reluctantly, unable to think of any more questions. I knew I was being thrown out for the second time in twelve hours. "You must come and try the tearoom properly. I have a ten per cent discount for Sidmouth residents."

Susan clapped her hands. "Delightful. I'll come soon. Let me see you out."

Seconds later, I stood on the pavement outside Susan's house, marvelling at how quickly I'd been pushed out. Susan had done it very politely, but her expression – no, her whole demeanour – had changed as soon as I asked whether she socialised with Larry. There was definitely something going on, but it wasn't as if I could knock on the door again.

I decided there was only one thing I could do to find out more: ask my friend Holly.

CHAPTER 16

I popped home for the ring, then stopped off at Holly's shop. Holly's Craft Corner was a stalwart of the Sidmouth high street. I loved Holly's shop: in fact, if I hadn't had a scheme to open my own tearoom, I'd have begged Holly to take me on as staff. There was something so comforting about the place.

Holly had opened her shop ten years ago, initially with just a few products, but it had grown and now had a wide choice of stock. Holly also had a natural connection with her customers and an uncanny knack of stocking items that tourists liked.

When I entered, a symphony of colour and texture greeted me. The shelves were lined with an array of vibrant fabrics, spools of thread, and baskets of knitting yarn in every hue imaginable. To the right, a wooden rack displayed painting supplies – brushes, canvases, and tubes of acrylic and oil paint. Towards the back was an alcove dedicated to scrapbooking, with patterned papers, stamps, and stickers neatly organised. Glass jars filled with buttons, beads, and other small items stood on a rustic wooden table.

I found Holly busy checking her stock of wool, clipboard

in hand. She had a wide range of high-quality wool, much of which she hand-dyed herself, in the back of the shop.

"Hello, darling." I kissed Holly on the cheek. "I've got a question for you. What do you know about Susan Mason and Larry?"

Holly put the clipboard down. "Susan Mason? I know very little about her. I've hardly ever spoken to her, but the word on the street is that she was having an affair with Larry."

"Hmm. That makes sense. Did you know about this before?"

"Before what?"

"Before the murder?"

"Before and after."

It never failed to amaze me how Holly knew so much gossip. Yet she wasn't the gossiping kind: she never whispered about others. People just seemed to tell her things.

"Do you know why people think they're having an affair? Was there proof?"

Holly looked up at the shelves of wool, her eyes scanning the multicoloured skeins. "Nobody has proof of anything, but they gossip about it anyway. Someone probably saw them talking one day and jumped to conclusions."

"So no proof at all, then."

"No. But more than one person has mentioned it to me."

A customer came in, and I realised I should make myself scarce. "Thanks, Holly, I'll see you later."

———

I returned to the tearoom the long way round, via the seafront. It was a clear, bright day with the promise of sunshine and no wind. The English Channel was almost perfectly still, and I paused for a moment to take in the sea.

I'd missed living by the sea in London, despite all the diversions and things to do there. I was glad to be back home.

"This is lovely," Lady Camilla commented. "There's nothing like sea air."

"You can smell?" I asked.

"Of course. We can see and smell."

"What about taste and touch?"

"Neither of those, we don't need to eat."

We strolled down the esplanade and were nearing my tearoom when we reached one of the beach shelters, a wooden structure built in the Victorian era and still steadfast, despite the seawater and wind that had been thrown at it over the years. I glanced at the figure sitting inside and stopped when I saw it was DI O'Malley.

He looked up as I was about to pass. "Hello," he said, smiling.

Lily swooped in and sat next to him on the bench. "Oooh, it's DI Handsome." She gazed up at him.

"Hello." I paused, not sure whether to walk on or stay and talk.

He indicated the seat next to him, and before I knew it I was sitting down, with Lily separating us.

"Quite the spot for contemplation," I remarked, looking out to sea.

He glanced at me and smiled, then looked at the view. "Indeed. I've always loved the seaside."

"Did you live near the sea where you grew up in Ireland?"

"Not too close. Our biggest waves were in the bathtub. Killarney is in the southwest of Ireland. It's under an hour to the nearest seaside town, but we didn't go much. It's right next to a huge lake, though."

"So you're no stranger to a paddleboard?"

"Not a paddleboard, but I did some canoeing." He paused for a moment. "Did the reopening of the tearoom go well?"

"Yes! I'll be opening in about half an hour." I looked at my watch.

"Glad to hear it."

"Any updates?"

He exhaled. "It's a tangled web, but we're making progress. Slowly."

"Don't you think it's strange that Larry's old business partner came to town to find him? He threatened to kill him just a few minutes before he was murdered."

Lily, who was still sitting between us, looked at O'Malley for an answer, then back at me. I gave her a stern look to say *go away,* and she took the hint, tutting to herself, then floating towards the sea.

"It is odd, yes, and I have interviewed him," O'Malley said.

"But you would have charged him if you thought he'd done it." It was a statement, not a question.

He turned to me again and raised his eyebrows. "I would have, yes."

"So he had a motive. What was his motive?"

O'Malley sighed. "I'm sorry, I can't tell you that."

"I tried asking him myself, but he slammed the door in my face."

"Did you now? Why are you so keen on finding out?"

"He made a scene at the opening of my tearoom, and the person he made a scene with was murdered."

He gave a sort of chuckle. "We don't usually arrest people for making scenes. That's reserved for really bad theatre. But when you put it like that, it's no wonder you're surprised that I haven't arrested him." I waited for him to say more, but he didn't.

"He's being very elusive," Lily said, as she floated back. She raised her arms a little and I felt a warm breeze.

I looked at her, then at O'Malley. "Well, I'd better get going. The tearoom won't open itself."

O'Malley nodded. "See you."

Lily floated up to me. "You're annoyed with him."

"Of course I am. He wouldn't tell me anything! It's very frustrating. Anyway..." I narrowed my eyes at Lily. "You moved your arms and made the wind blow on us."

Lily looked away and giggled.

"You did! I knew it."

"Now you know that I can make the wind blow."

I started walking back to the tearoom. "How much?"

"A gentle breeze is easy. The stronger the wind, the harder it is for me."

The other ghosts appeared and walked with us. "Lily likes to blow out candles at birthday parties," Mr Darby said, in a severe tone. "She once upset a six-year-old boy so much that he refused to have candles on his birthday cake until he was eighteen.

Lady Camilla scowled. "The poor boy was distraught. It was a terrible trick to play."

I looked at Lily, who had an angelic expression on her face. She clearly regretted nothing.

By the time I arrived at the tearoom, I had decided that if O'Malley would not tell me David's motive and why he was off the hook, I would find out from David himself. And this time, I would not take no for an answer. But I'd have to do it later, when the tearoom was closed.

CHAPTER 17

was so busy in the tearoom that I hardly had time to think about visiting David, especially when a large group of people arrived just after noon: eight women and two men, all in Regency costume. I stood watching them in amazement and they filed in.

Carol went over to the group. I pulled myself together and joined her.

"Hello!" said a middle-aged lady in a pale-yellow gown. She wore a straw bonnet with a matching yellow ribbon. "Do you have enough room for all of us? If not, we'd love to have a look around anyway. We've been dying to come here ever since we heard about it."

"Er…" I looked at the others in the group, each wearing a hopeful smile. "Yes, of course. We're fairly quiet at the moment, so if you can wait a few minutes I'll move some tables together."

"Marvellous!" The lady beamed. "We're from the Jane Austen Appreciation Society of Devon, and we just couldn't wait to come and see your tearoom."

"How have I never heard about you before today?" I felt some trepidation. If the Jane Austen Appreciation Society of

Devon didn't like my tearoom, I could be in trouble. Everything had to be just so for them.

Then Mr Wickers caught my eye. He was inspecting the group one by one. "Heavens, more Jane Austen fans! Mr Darby, come and look!" He beckoned him over.

Mr Darby sat brooding, looking out of the window. He turned, sighed, then looked out of the window again.

"He's in one of his dark moments," Mr Wickers explained.

I went to move the tables while the group busied themselves exploring the gift shop and taking selfies.

When they were seated I gave them menus, and straight away they commented on the Jane Austen-themed names. I left them to decide and went into the kitchen to tell Emma, who couldn't resist peeking at them. "This is amazing!" she said. "Make sure we get a photo of them all before they leave. It'll be great publicity on social media."

"Don't worry, I intend to!"

All the ghosts except Mr Darby were now inspecting the group. Mr Collingwood and Mr Wickers were in deep conversation about what the two men were wearing. They were in classic gentlemen's attire for the Regency period: breeches, long jackets, and a shirt with a cravat. I thought they looked very dashing. Meanwhile, Lady Camilla and Lily were inspecting the ladies and commenting on their dresses and hair.

I shook my head, smiling. When I had imagined what the first few weeks in the tearoom would be like, I had never envisaged a group of ghosts milling around with a crowd of Jane Austen fans. But I liked it, and maybe other fan groups would visit, too.

The Jane Austen fan group turned out to be a lively bunch, filling the tearoom with laughter and animated conversation for nearly three hours. Not content with just one pot of tea, they sampled lots of items on the menu.

They were also fond of the Austen-themed gifts. One man

bought a set of *Pride and Prejudice* coasters. "These will be perfect for my 'Mr Darcy Drinking Game'," he said. "One sip every time he broods!"

They all stood together for photos, and many of the women posed by the framed pictures of Austen heroes, pretending to swoon and fanning themselves with vintage handkerchiefs for comedic effect.

When they left, the till was pleasantly full. It was clear they'd enjoyed their experience as much as I'd enjoyed hosting them.

After the excitement of the day, I was exhausted when it got to closing time. Only then did I remember that I wanted to visit David again. So it was late when I finally got changed and walked to Pebbles B&B. The front door was wedged open. I entered, went upstairs and was standing outside the door of room seven before I'd even thought to speak to Meg, the owner.

I paused and the ghosts passed through the door. A moment later, Mr Darby's face appeared through the wall. "He's in. Watching television."

I nearly jumped out of my skin. I took a deep breath and knocked hard on the door. A moment later, David opened it. He sighed when he saw me. All the ghosts were behind him.

"You again," he said. "What do you want this time? Still after an apology?"

"No. Look, can we talk downstairs in the living room?"

He pondered, then nodded. "I've been in this room too long, and I haven't spoken to many people lately, so you're in luck."

We made our way downstairs to the guests' living room. It was small, despite the bay window, but had an inviting glow. The sand-coloured sofa with contrasting scatter cushions complemented the driftwood coffee table. On the walls, framed watercolours showed Sidmouth's red cliffs and beach.

I waited for David to sit down, then took the sofa opposite, the coffee table separating us. The ghosts remained silent as they waited for the conversation to start.

I wondered whether I should begin with some small talk about the weather, but decided to dive right in. "I hear you were questioned at length by the police."

"I was. But as you can see, they haven't arrested me." David snorted. "Stupid plod. I left the tearoom at least ten minutes before he was murdered."

I thought it had been more like five minutes. I cast my mind back to the day of the opening. Had I seen Larry alive and well after David had left? Yes, I had. "Yes, I saw you leave."

"Did you tell the police that?"

"Of course."

He gave me a nod of approval.

"Where did you go after you left?"

"I wandered around town, then came back here." His eyes narrowed. "I told the police all this. That's why they haven't charged me. They've got no evidence because I didn't do it."

"What were you arguing over?"

"Is that why you're here digging? You're very persistent." He paused, contemplating.

I shrugged. "I'm trying to get to the bottom of the mystery. It's affecting my dream of the tearoom. I want it solved. If you're nothing to do with Larry's death, then I can focus on what is."

That convinced him. "I suppose you might as well know. Larry had an affair with my daughter. She was eighteen at the time and she was in a vulnerable place. He used her. He abused his position and betrayed me."

"When did this happen?"

"Five years ago. He moved to Sidmouth to get away from the shame of what he'd done."

"Is that why you came here, to confront him?"

David rubbed his eyes. "Yes."

"But why wait five years?"

"Because he contacted my daughter again."

That was a powerful motive to kill someone. But O'Malley hadn't arrested David, so he must be sure he was innocent. "Go on," I said.

"He sent my daughter a private message on social media a few weeks ago. It upset her. Even though she's twenty-three now, she still hasn't got over what happened all those years ago. She came to realise he'd groomed her. I came here to stop him contacting her again."

Lady Camilla spoke. "That makes sense, but it's a powerful motive for murder."

"How long have you been in Sidmouth?" I asked.

"I got here a few days before I confronted him in your tearoom. I was biding my time. While I waited, I spoke to Debbie before I came to Sidmouth, but she didn't do anything. She knew about the affair five years ago and she forgave him. I wanted her to tell him to stop, but she was useless."

"What did she say?"

"She said the messages were just friendly and there was nothing in them."

Lady Camilla scoffed. "A likely story."

I looked over at her. She was standing near the window, and I hadn't noticed her come in.

"That seems unlikely," I said to David.

"I know. I hired a private detective, who found Larry here in Sidmouth, and I decided to take matters into my own hands."

I felt a lot of sympathy for David and his daughter. The unwanted attentions of an older man were not something which any young woman should have to put up with. If I'd had a daughter, I would have done the same thing.

"So that's the reason why your business partnership broke up?"

"Yes. And it's why they moved from Kent to here. But look here. As much as I wanted to, I didn't touch Larry."

"Why did you choose my opening ceremony to confront him?"

David sighed and rubbed his face again. "Are you still after that apology? Well, I'd given up on Debbie doing anything to stand in Larry's way, so I decided I'd have to step in. I followed them into the tearoom, and I saw him sitting there drinking tea and eating cakes as though he owned the place and a word from him would bring success or failure. It made me so mad that I couldn't contain it any longer."

David fell silent. His face had turned red and he was breathing hard, trying to get himself under control. Finally, he focused on me. "I've nothing else to say. As soon as the police let me, I'll leave."

I nodded and stood up. "I understand. What he did was inexcusable. Thank you for talking to me." Part of me wanted to air my own grievances about Larry, but despite everything, no one deserves to be killed.

Outside, I mused that if he was telling the truth, someone else had an even stronger motive to kill Larry. Maybe it was Debbie, because she'd had enough of Larry going after younger women. Maybe this wasn't the only time he'd done it.

CHAPTER 18

That evening, I decided I needed to stop obsessing about the murder and searched the internet for any information about the two pubs that might have Black-Eye Elmore's treasure map.

I sat on the sofa cross-legged, with Mr Collingwood and Lady Camilla.

The first pub was the the Swan Inn, in the centre of the town, but on a back street. "Do you have any idea where in the pubs the map might be?" I asked.

Lady Camilla sniffed. "No, it could be anywhere. But we can search the tavern if you enter it, since we can pass between walls. I'm afraid you must go right inside the public house."

I stood up. "All right, let's go. No point in waiting."

Ten minutes later, I stood outside the Swan Inn with the ghosts. Its traditional, welcoming exterior was painted white, making it stand out compared to the surrounding buildings. A large, simple sign hung above the entrance, displaying the name of the pub and an image of a swan. Inside, the bar was cosy and traditional. Above the dark-wood bar hung glasses and bottles, ready for service. The back wall of the bar had a colourful display of drink options.

Lady Camilla addressed the others. "We need to go through this building with a fine-tooth comb. Mr Collingwood, you're with me. We'll start with the attic and the upper floors. Lily and Mr Wickers, you go to the cellar. Darby, you start here in the bar area." The ghosts disappeared through the walls, ceilings and floors.

I went to the bar and ordered a glass of red wine, then took it to a table, pulled out the book about smuggling and started to read.

A few pages in, I felt a familiar tingle. Mr Wickers and Lily rose through the floor to join Mr Darby.

I buried myself in the book again and only looked up when I felt a gust of wind from the main door. O'Malley was coming in – and he was with a woman.

I looked about frantically. I didn't want him to see me drinking in a pub on my own. Hastily, I lifted the book so that it was in front of my face and tried to read, though I wasn't taking any of it in.

I heard him order drinks and the woman giggled. I peered over my book at her. She was about thirty and very pretty, with long brown hair, dressed in smart jeans and a crop top.

I tried not to be insanely jealous, but it was hard. Then again, what did I have to be jealous of? There was no way that a man like O'Malley would be interested in me when he was with someone as gorgeous as her.

Before I could raise the book again, O'Malley looked over and saw me. *Oh dear.*

"Trinity?"

I groaned inside. That was all I needed. Now he really would think I was a sad, middle-aged woman drinking alone.

I raised the book again, hoping he'd think I hadn't heard him.

"Trinity?" His voice was closer now. "It *is* you. How are you this evening?"

He was standing in front of my table. I put the book down. "Oh, hello," I said, trying to sound surprised. "I'm very well, thank you."

"Come out for a drink, I see." He looked at the wine glass. "And reading a book, too." He turned it round to read the title. "A book about smuggling in Sidmouth? Interesting. I hope you're not getting any ideas." He laughed.

"I, er…" *He's joking, right?* He did have a smile on his face. I looked over at his companion, who was still at the bar.

He followed my gaze. "That's my sister Ciara. She's over from Ireland visiting. It's great to see her."

Relief washed over me. His sister!

"Ciara, come and meet Trinity."

Ciara strolled over, and I wondered if there were any ugly members of the O'Malley family. I doubted it. She was even more stunning close up.

"Hi," I squeaked.

"Hi," she replied with a smile.

"Trinity owns the Jane Austen tearoom," O'Malley explained.

Ciara nodded. "The one with the murder? Cormac told me about it."

"I thought you weren't allowed to talk about it to civilians?" I took a sip of my wine.

"Only what's known to the public." Was he blushing? His cheeks were definitely pinker than a moment ago.

There was a long, awkward silence, and Ciara nudged O'Malley. He jumped slightly. "Well, have a good evening. Enjoy your book." They moved to a table nearby and sat down.

I lifted the book up and concentrated hard on it, not reading a word.

Twenty minutes later, all of the ghosts reappeared. "We've

searched high and low, under every floorboard and in every crevice and corner, and found nothing," said Lady Camilla.

"We found plenty of things – just not the map." Mr Wickers winked at me.

"Hush!" scolded Lady Camilla. "We shall not talk about what we saw in the attic."

I finished my wine and stood up. "We'll have to try the Volunteer pub another time," I murmured. "That must be where the map is hidden."

CHAPTER 19

The next day, the tearoom was busy again. Lily floated up to me at the till after I had finished taking payment from a customer. "I have great news!" she exclaimed. "Mr Wickers overheard a customer say that the eminent scholar Dr Laura Warwick is coming to the tearoom today! The customer read about it on the computer." She clapped her hands together.

"Which customer was it?" I asked, looking around. "Are they still here?"

"No, he left."

"I wonder why he didn't tell me himself?" I thought back to all the customers who'd been in that day. Who could it have been?

"That's because it's supposed to be secret squirrel. She gets recognised wherever she goes and she hates it."

"But if she hates being recognised, why is she telling everyone on the internet where she's going?"

Lily shrugged.

I went to the kitchen and Lily followed. "How does Mr Wickers know about Dr Laura Warwick?" I asked. "She's one of the country's most famous Jane Austen scholars. She has over four million subscribers to her video channel, you know... Well, I don't suppose you do. I can't wait to meet her if she really is coming here! She knows everything about Jane Austen."

Lily's eyebrows shot up. "She doesn't know that Jane based the book on us."

"You're right. And if I told her, she wouldn't believe me."

"No one would believe you unless you let them put on the ring. But even then, we ghosts don't have to appear to the ring-holder."

"I need to make sure everything is perfect for her visit. Do I look all right?" I smoothed down my dress and checked my hair.

Lady Camilla appeared and inspected me. "You look flustered and tired, but otherwise acceptable."

I shook my head. "Acceptable isn't good enough. I'll change into my best dress. I was keeping it for a special occasion, and this is definitely special. Laura Warwick, visiting my tearoom!"

I could hardly believe it. For one thing, she lived in Oxford, which was hours and hours from Devon. Surely she hadn't come all that way just to see my tearoom. No, she must be on holiday here.

More and more customers came in. I kept an eye out for Dr Laura, but by late afternoon she hadn't appeared. There was another visitor, however: Susan Mason. She was with a female friend, and I seated them by the window. If I wanted more information from her, I would have to butter her up a little. Maybe I should give her free cake: that might make her open up.

They ordered Mrs Bennet's Afternoon Tea. It began with a selection of sandwiches: cucumber and cream cheese on soft white bread and egg and watercress on wholemeal bread. To follow, a classic plain scone, served warm with clotted cream and strawberry jam, a lemon-lavender shortbread, a mini raspberry tart and a special touch: a small glass of "Nervous Tonic", a refreshing rosewater, garnished with a leaf of fresh pepper-mint. I'd come up with the idea of the nervous tonic myself and spent hours picking out the right green Victorian-style glasses.

I didn't get the chance to talk to Susan alone until almost an hour later, when her friend visited the bathroom. I made a beeline for the table and sat down opposite Susan.

"This is such a lovely tearoom," said Susan, and adjusted her teacup.

"Thank you." I leaned forward. "Look, I heard a rumour. Something you might want to know about."

Susan picked up her cup and sipped her tea.

"It's about you and Larry."

The cup stayed steady, but Susan's eyebrows rose. She put her cup down. "What sort of rumour might that be?"

"Does it need spelling out?"

"Clearly."

I leaned forward as far as I could. "People say that you were having an affair," I murmured.

Susan gave an almost imperceptible shake of the head. "Gosh, those rumours just won't go away, will they? Fine. Yes, we were having an affair, no, he wouldn't leave his wife for me, and no, I didn't murder him because of it. I ended it, actually. It was a stupid thing to do. Have an affair with Larry, I mean. We often had to work late together, and one night it just, well, happened. And then the next, and so on. It became a habit. But his wife got suspicious and I told him we had to stop."

I hadn't expected her to admit it so freely. "Oh."

Susan chuckled. "I know what you're thinking. He wasn't exactly attractive and he was grumpy as hell. But I was lonely and he was in the right place at the right time. I saw sense quickly, though. Happy, now?"

I stared at her. "Happy?"

"That you know my little secret."

"Sorry. I'm just trying to find out who committed the murder."

"And you want to eliminate me from your list of suspects?" Susan smiled. "Trinity, why don't you leave finding the murderer to the handsome detective, and get on with running this lovely tearoom?"

"She does have a point," said Mr Darby, who was floating near the table.

I shrugged. "Maybe I should."

Susan leaned across the table and took my hand. "Be a dear and keep what I've told you to yourself, please. People in this town never forget any indiscretions, and I could do with retaining my dignity, such as it is."

I nodded. "I'll keep your secret."

"Thank you."

Back in the kitchen, I sighed. Yes, I should leave investigating to the police, but it was very hard. I needed the murder cleared up. I couldn't move on from it. I knew it was stupid, but I was becoming obsessed. An unsolved murder was hanging over my tearoom like a dark cloud and spoiling my dream. And Dr Laura Warwick still hadn't come in. I was starting to think that she wouldn't visit at all.

Mr Darby floated into the kitchen. "Her friend has returned from the ladies' room."

"She took that better than I thought she would."

"She wanted you to keep it a secret, though."

"I'm not surprised. We've all had our indiscretions."

Mr Darby adjusted his cravat. "I haven't. I'm shocked at the depravity I encounter these days."

"It still happened when you were alive – you just didn't talk about it. Anyway, didn't a fine gentleman like you do anything bad? You must have had opportunities. You know... an attractive widow, a kitchen maid…"

Mr Darby looked affronted. "Of course not. How rude!" He floated rapidly away.

"Wait!" I called, but it was too late. Mr Darby had vanished into the ether, leaving me to ponder the moral standards of ghosts.

Just then, the doorbell rang. That meant new customers and possibly Dr Laura.

CHAPTER 20

popped my head out of the kitchen to take a look. This time it was Debbie, accompanied by two men I didn't recognise. My conversation with Mr Darby forgotten, I approached them.

The two men accompanying Debbie were a study in contrasts. One was tall and bulky, his light-grey suit and white shirt barely containing his protruding belly. The other was shorter, wearing a casual navy-blue jacket over a white T-shirt and jeans.

"Debbie, how are you?" I asked, in a sympathetic tone. "I must admit that I'm surprised to see you here. I thought the tearoom might hold bad memories for you." The moment the words were out of my mouth, I regretted them.

Debbie looked flustered. "Well, yes, I suppose it does."

Hoping I wasn't blushing, I turned to the men. "I don't believe we've met."

Debbie introduced them. "This is Clive Hayward, Larry's business partner," she said, indicating the larger man. "And Larry's cousin, Victor."

"Nice to meet you both."

"Larry owns – I mean, owned – half of Bloomhaven Garden Centre with Clive," Debbie explained.

"Oh, really? I love it there. When I moved into my house, the garden was a mess. I've been spending lots of money there."

"I'm very proud of the place," said Clive. "We bought it when it was a run-down mess five years ago, and I've built it up to its current glory."

"And Larry helped," Debbie murmured.

"He did, in his own way," said Clive. "I was the one with the vision and the plan. He invested the money."

"A sleeping partner. Sounds ideal." I'd used my own money for the tearoom: I didn't want anyone to interfere with my vision. I had needed a small bank loan, but if all went to plan, that would be paid off in three years.

I led them to a table at the back and handed them menus.

"Are you in Sidmouth to pay your respects?" I asked Victor.

"I am. Terrible what happened. And it was here?"

I nodded. "In the garden."

Victor sighed. "Poor Larry. Such a shame."

"Poor Debbie, too." I gave Debbie a conciliatory smile.

Clive studied the menu. "I'll have the cream tea with plain scones and a pot of English breakfast tea."

"I'll just have a pot of tea," said Debbie.

Victor glanced at the menu. "I'll have the same as Clive."

As I wrote down their orders, Lady Camilla floated over. I had to bite my tongue when she began tutting at Debbie.

In the kitchen, I asked her what was wrong.

"A widow must wear black, especially in public!" she exclaimed. "What is the world coming to?"

"That tradition stopped a long time ago."

"I know. That doesn't make it right."

A few minutes later, I took out their orders. Before I could walk away, Clive asked, "Have you heard how the police investigation is going?"

I shrugged. "Debbie will know more than me."

Debbie was gazing out of the window but turned at the sound of her name. "What?" she said. "Oh, they just said investigations were ongoing."

Clive frowned and looked at me. "But aren't they keeping you up to date, too? I mean, you own the tearoom where the murder took place."

"No, they're not."

"Really?" said Victor. "But I suppose you hardly knew Larry."

"That's right. But when we did interact, it was antagonistic. On his side, mind, not mine."

"Yes, he had strong views about this place." Clive chuckled. "He mentioned it a few times."

"I couldn't understand his opposition at the time," I said. "Now that I know he part-owned the garden centre, it makes sense."

"How so?" said Clive.

"He didn't want his – your – customers coming here instead of visiting the café at the garden centre."

Clive waved that away. "I was never worried about that. The garden centre's on the other side of town, and we have a completely different clientele. I get the locals; you get the tourists. More or less anyway."

"Exactly!" I exclaimed. I was starting to like Clive.

"Larry was so foolish in some ways. Sorry, Victor, I know he's your family, but he was at times."

Victor shrugged. He didn't seem to disagree.

"But not in everything," Debbie put in. I'd almost forgotten she was there.

I smiled at Clive. "If I'd met you before today, Clive, I would have invited you to the opening ceremony."

He smiled back. "I would have loved to come, but I was away on business."

"Well, I hope you enjoy your scones and tea. If there's anything else you need, let me know."

Debbie, Victor and Clive eventually left, after going out to the garden for a short while. I supposed they were remembering Larry and reflecting on his last moments.

I looked at the clock. It was ten minutes till closing time and Dr Laura had not appeared. Maybe she had got stuck in traffic, or something else had come up. But I had to admit that I was disappointed. I'd read several of her books and watched her documentaries on TV, all about Jane Austen.

I pressed the turquoise stone in the centre of my ring and felt a prickling sensation.

Lady Camilla appeared by the till. "What is it?" she snapped. "I was asleep."

"I want to speak to Mr Wickers."

"Mr Wickers? Why?"

"Just get him, will you?"

Lady Camilla mumbled something and vanished. A moment later, Mr Wickers appeared.

"I've been waiting to meet Dr Laura Warwick all day but she's not here," I said. "What exactly did you hear from the customer who said she was coming in?"

Mr Wickers blinked. "Dr who?"

"Dr Warwick."

"I have no idea who you're talking about."

I put my hands on my hips and narrowed my eyes. "Fetch Lily, please."

Lily appeared a moment later. "How can I help?"

"Mr Wickers claims to know nothing about Dr Laura Warwick visiting the tearoom today."

Lily looked from me to Mr Wickers, then back again, and burst out laughing. Mr Wickers joined in.

I gave them my best Paddington Bear hard stare. "So you made that up, about her visiting?"

"I'm sorry, we couldn't resist it." Mr Wickers sniggered.

I sighed. While I was normally a good sport about jokes at my expense, today I wasn't in the mood. I turned to Lady Camilla. "Have they done this sort of thing before?"

She sighed. "A few times, I'm afraid."

I scowled at them. "I'll get you back, you know. You'd better watch out!"

Mr Wickers made a deep bow. "I look forward to it."

I was about to turn the sign to Closed when the bell above the door tinkled and DI O'Malley entered.

CHAPTER 21

"Hi," O'Malley said, closing the door behind him. He looked me up and down. "Nice dress. Isn't that different from the one you were wearing the other day?"

"It is. I'm impressed that you noticed."

Lady Camilla swooped across the tearoom. "He's a policeman: he's supposed to notice things like that."

"Would you like a cup of tea?" I asked.

"Thank you, yes." He pronounced thank you as "tank you". I liked it.

"Take a seat, and I'll be back in a mo."

I went to the kitchen and returned a few minutes later with a tray of tea things and two scones. O'Malley was standing by the small-gift area, looking at one of the special-edition *Pride and Prejudice* hardbacks. The ghosts were gathered around him.

"I thought you might like some scones to go with your tea." I put the tray on a nearby table.

"An excellent idea," said Lady Camilla. "He's far too thin. Needs fattening up." The other ghosts nodded.

O'Malley smiled, closed the book and came over. "Thanks.

I skipped lunch, and I'm as hungry as a pirate who's lost his treasure map to the kitchen."

I laughed, then sat down at the table. "I make all the scones myself."

"Do you buy in the other cakes?"

"I get some from a local bakery, but I make the Devon apple cake myself, too."

"I'll have to try that next time."

He cut open a scone, put clotted cream and then jam on it, and took a bite.

I nodded in approval. "You've only just moved to Devon and already you're learning our Devon ways."

"Cream first, always. It's how we do it in my part of Ireland, too."

I poured tea for us both. "I've never been to Ireland. Do you go often?"

"Now and again, to see my mam."

I offered the milk to O'Malley, who took it. "So, how can I help you?"

"Just keeping you up to date with everything. And to tell you, you're not a suspect."

"That's gratifying. Thank you for telling me." I smiled and wondered if O'Malley usually told people if they were, and then weren't, suspects.

"Seeing as the murder happened in your tearoom, I thought you deserved to know."

"What made you realise I was innocent?"

"About thirty other people who never saw you leave the main tearoom."

"Sounds good to me." I took a sip of tea and smiled at him over the rim of the cup. "Clive Hayward was in the tearoom earlier: he came in with Debbie. Have you spoken to him?"

"Are you questioning my ability to detect?" said O'Malley, in mock indignation. "My detection skills are so good, even my shadow takes notes."

"Of course not. I just wondered."

"I have spoken to him, actually."

"I didn't know Larry owned half of Bloomhaven," I said.

"Larry has – I mean, had – an interesting past."

I leaned forward. "Is Clive your prime suspect?"

"No. He has an iron-clad alibi, too. He was away on business."

"I suppose Debbie gets all Larry's assets, now that he's dead."

"I can't discuss his will, Trinity. But if you do a simple search for Bloomhaven Garden Centre on the *Companies House* website, you'll see that Clive and Larry owned half each. Neither of them has any children."

"So Debbie will inherit Larry's half, which is probably why Clive's schmoozing her."

"Tea and scones in a tearoom isn't exactly schmoozing."

I shook my head. "There's so much gossip floating round about Larry and anyone who knew him. It's unreal."

"And I've said more than I should. I'm not supposed to discuss ongoing cases with members of the public."

"It's a shame you can't tell me more, DI O'Malley. I want to find out who did it as much as you do. I've had ghost hunters in here, you know, trying to connect with Larry's ghost. They were really annoying."

He smiled. "Did they buy anything?"

"I told them they could only stay if they did. They went into the garden to connect with what's left of Larry's essence and find out who killed him. It's utterly ridiculous."

"Yup. It's not as if ghosts exist." He took another bite of his scone. "Mmm, this is really good."

Until he said that, the ghosts had been keeping a low profile at the other end of the tearoom. Lily floated up to the table. "Did he just say that ghosts don't exist?"

"He did." Mr Collingwood folded his arms and stared at

O'Malley. "Let's hope he's more perceptive about criminals than he is about the afterlife."

O'Malley's phone rang and he checked the screen. "Sorry, got to get this. Hi. Yes… Okay"

I stood up and moved to the other side of the tearoom to give him privacy.

"He could be your Mr Darcy," Mr Wickers said, with a mischievous wink.

O'Malley looked up from his phone and caught my eye. He smiled, and I felt a warm tingling sensation in the pit of my stomach.

Lily giggled. "Ooh, you've got a secret blend of feelings brewing for him."

I bit my lip. "Is it that obvious?"

O'Malley ended the call. I went back to the table, my cheeks warm.

"Sorry about that," he said. "Duty calls, but I really enjoyed our chat. If I don't solve this case, at least I've solved the mystery of the best scones." He gave me a lingering look which made me feel even warmer.

As O'Malley left, Lily and Mr Wickers hovered near me. "I think he's smitten," Lily said, her expression dreamy.

"Do you think so?" I said. "Maybe he was just being friendly. Maybe he's like that with everyone." *Every woman.*

Mr Darby's deep voice cut through my thoughts. "A gentleman should never lead a lady on if he is not serious."

I nodded emphatically. "I totally agree."

CHAPTER 22

That evening, I got out my laptop. Instead of opening the accounts software, which was usually my only reason for logging on, I searched the internet for details of Larry's business dealings. I was working under the watchful eye of Mr Wickers, who was sitting next to me on the sofa.

"I was definitely born at the wrong time," he remarked. "These computer machines are very helpful."

"I'm not very good with computers, but I can do the basics," I replied.

"Ooh, what is that?" He leaned forward and pointed.

"It's a website."

He laughed. "A site made of webs? What is the use of that?"

"How long has it been since you saw a computer?"

Mr Wickers looked at me. "A few years."

"How many? Five? Ten? Two?"

"I can't say."

"Why not?"

"If I told you, it would give away details of a previous ring-owner."

"I still think that's a stupid rule."

Mr Wickers sighed. "As we've said before, we saw most of what the previous ring-owners got up to. We made a gentlemen's agreement not to pass that on."

"You're a gentleman?"

Mr Wickers gasped. "How dare you think otherwise?" he spluttered, and adjusted his cravat. *That hit a nerve*, I thought, and made a mental note in case it would be useful in the future.

"I'm sorry if I offended you," I said. "It's just that in *Pride and Prejudice*, your character basically kidnaps a teenage girl."

He stuck his nose in the air. "I would never have done such a thing. I did not approve of that particular plot development."

"I'm glad to hear it."

He examined the screen. "What are you doing?"

"I'm looking at company records on a government website."

"Who are you looking for?"

"*What* am I looking for, you mean. I'm about to look for Bloomhaven Garden Centre, which is up the road." I typed in the name and pressed *Search*.

Moments later, the screen updated. "Ah, here it is... Bloomhaven Garden Centre. DI O'Malley is right: Clive and Larry own half each."

I continued searching, then frowned. "This is strange. David, who had that fight with Larry, said they'd been in business together, but there's no record of it here."

"The computer keeps historic records, too?" Mr Wickers said. "If there is no record of it, and the computer is correct, then perhaps the gentleman in question was lying."

"Or it wasn't an official arrangement."

"Or he used another name." Mr Wickers pondered this. "That's what I would do: become untraceable. Especially if I – I mean, he – moved across the country."

I considered the options. "I think you're right. I'll try and find out if Larry ever changed his name."

"An excellent idea!" Mr Wickers exclaimed, and beamed at me. "How will you do that?"

"I haven't a clue."

CHAPTER 23

The next morning, before opening the tearoom, I went to see Holly in her craft shop. I had to wait a few minutes, as Holly was serving a customer, but once the shop was quiet, I told her about O'Malley's visit and what I'd discovered from my internet research.

"Sounds like you're becoming a detective." Holly grinned at me from behind the counter. "Ever thought about joining the police?"

"No! And I'm too old, anyway."

"What, at forty-two? Are you sure?"

"I'm not bothering to find out: I'm happy with my tearoom. Anyway, what's the latest you've heard about the murder?"

"No more than you."

"That's disappointing."

"I know. Except the word on the street is that Larry's cousin has turned up in town because Larry left him money in his will."

"Really? I met him yesterday. He came in the tearoom with Debbie. How do you know he has an inheritance?"

She shrugged. "People tell me things. I have my sources." She tapped the side of her nose.

Sometimes it felt as if Holly's sources were everyone in town. Information just seemed to fall into her lap. Maybe she'd be better as the detective.

I frowned. "It's very suspicious that Victor suddenly arrives just after Larry was murdered, even if he's due to inherit a lot of money. Did he really arrive yesterday? Maybe he arrived *before* Larry was murdered. If so, he's a prime suspect!" My mind raced as I considered this.

"But he wasn't at your opening," Holly said, bringing me back to reality.

I sighed. "You're right, but it's still suspicious."

"Greedy, perhaps, but not suspicious. I can't understand any married couple who doesn't leave their entire fortune, big or small, to the other partner or children. Strange, that."

"We don't know who is going to inherit from Larry."

I thought about my situation with my ex-husband, Dean. When our son, Oliver, was born, we wrote wills leaving everything to each other if one of us died. If we died together somehow, Oliver would inherit everything. It had felt like the natural thing to do. Since the divorce, I'd made a new will and left everything to Oliver.

"Is Victor staying with Debbie?" I asked.

"No, he's at the Royal Hotel."

The Royal was one of the more expensive hotels in the town. If Victor was short of money, he wouldn't be staying there, unless he was the sort of person who lived his life on credit.

Kate, who owned the art shop on the other side of Holly's craft shop, popped her head round the door. "Something's kicking off outside. Want to come and see the fun?"

"What?" Holly came out from behind the counter and ran outside. I was on her heels.

Fifty feet away, in the town square, stood two women, one shouting at the other. I recognised Susan and Debbie.

"How could you?" Debbie shouted.

"Look, I don't know who you heard it from, but it's lies," said Susan. "Please don't make a scene."

"It's not lies! Everyone's talking about it. Everyone knows, and they're all laughing at me!"

"They're only laughing at you because you married such a ridiculous man," snapped Susan.

"You had an affair with him! Which of us is more ridiculous?" Debbie stabbed an accusatory finger at Susan.

"It was only for a few weeks, and then I finished it. I saw the light quickly. Unlike you."

"I knew it!" Debbie turned to the small crowd that had gathered. "Did you hear that, everyone?" She made a grab at Susan, and the crowd reacted with a mixture of gasps and laughter. I was agog. Debbie had always been so placid and meek.

"Let go of me!" Susan shouted.

Debbie was smaller than Susan, but her passion had given her extra oomph. She launched herself at Susan, grappling and clawing wildly. Susan tried to push her away, but Debbie clung on, nearly ripping Susan's blouse in her frenzy. They stumbled about, each struggling to overpower the other, their shrieks and curses filling the square. Debbie grabbed a fistful of Susan's hair and yanked violently, making Susan yelp. In retaliation, Susan scratched Debbie's arm.

The scuffle continued, both women now oblivious to the stunned crowd, focused only on inflicting pain. Debbie slapped Susan's face and she screamed.

"What do you think you're doing?" I shouted, suddenly realising that someone should intervene.

They ignored me. Susan used her longer reach to push Debbie away, but Debbie launched herself at her again.

I tried to pull Debbie away but she shook me off. How could a quiet, meek woman become so ferocious?

A tall, broad man from the crowd walked forward and pulled them apart. "Now, then, ladies. There's a time and place for fighting, and it's not now, or in public."

Debbie paused for a moment, catching her breath, then leaned round him and shouted, "I won't forget this, Susan. Watch out, if you know what's good for you. This isn't over." She stalked away.

Susan watched her go. "Yeah, Debbie, and you'll be sorry if you think this is over," she muttered. She straightened her rumpled clothes, shaking her head.

Then she looked up and saw me in the crowd. "You! You told her about the affair, and you said you wouldn't!"

"Me?" My eyes widened. "I didn't say a thing!"

"Really? So it's a complete coincidence that a few days after I tell you, Debbie finds out?" She stood with one hand on her hip, eyes narrowed in suspicion.

"I promise, I didn't."

Susan stared at me, stony-faced. "Well, I'm never coming to your tearoom again."

I sighed, unsure how to reply. Maybe it was for the best. If Susan did return, she would only cause a scene, and that would drive away customers.

"Show's over," Susan said to the few people still watching, and walked off.

Holly, who had been watching from farther back, came up to me. "That's why I never get involved in an argument."

"I'll know for next time," I said, with a rueful smile.

"Disgusting behaviour!" Lady Camilla said. "Brawling in the streets like common peasants. I've never seen anything like it!"

"They are common peasants," Mr Darby replied.

Lily giggled. "I thought it was hilarious. Women, fighting!"

I wanted to speak to them, but there were too many people near. I didn't want to gain a reputation for talking to myself. Instead, I walked to the tearoom. I had plenty to do before I could open up.

I started making a batch of chocolate brownies, watched by the ghosts.

Lady Camilla cleared her throat. "We have something to tell you."

I began mixing the butter into the flour. "Sounds serious."

Mr Wickers stepped forward. "We have a theory about who killed Larry."

That made me look up. "You do?"

"Yes. We think it was his wife."

"Debbie? What makes you think that?"

Mr Darby cleared his throat. "Well, the spouse is usually the murderer."

"I'm aware of that, but Debbie was in the tearoom with me and lots of other people when the murder happened. She couldn't have done it."

He held up a finger. "She could have slipped out. Or she could have done it just before or after everyone gathered inside."

"You've really been thinking about this, haven't you?"

"We don't get out much," said Lily, with a slight roll of her eyes. "Anything to relieve the boredom."

I considered. "Until this morning, I wouldn't have thought that Debbie had the physical strength to kill anyone. Now, though, having seen her attack Susan, I'd say she was more than capable. She was furious, too. I haven't seen her like that before."

"What would be her motive?" Lady Camilla asked.

"Inheriting the garden centre, of course," said Mr Darby.

"More like she wanted rid of him," said Lady Camilla, and sniffed. "Affairs, seduction, betrayal. It's no wonder he ended up dead."

"I've already spoken to her, though. She says she came into the tearoom for the opening ceremony, and she wasn't the last out of the garden. There were others behind her."

"That's what she says," said Mr Darby. "It doesn't mean it's true."

"All right, I'll have a word with her later and see if I can get her to talk about what happened, again. I'll say I'm concerned about her after the fight." That was true. I was more concerned about Susan, though. Debbie was vicious.

"Don't forget that you need to find out whether Larry ever changed his name," Mr Wickers reminded me.

"Yes, that, too."

CHAPTER 24

That evening, I locked up the tearoom and for the second time that week, pressed the buzzer for Debbie's flat.

There was no response.

I pressed it again, then knocked. Maybe Debbie was out.

I bent down and opened the letterbox flap. "Debbie, are you there?" As I leaned on the door, it gave way.

I pushed it open and hesitated a moment before entering. Lily followed me in, and the other ghosts stayed outside.

"Debbie?" I called. "Debbie?"

It felt strange, going into someone's home without being asked. But I needed answers. I stopped outside the lounge door, which was ajar, and looked in.

I gasped. Debbie was lying on the floor, her eyes open and staring.

There was no doubt that she was dead.

"Oh my goodness!" I moved forward and saw a pool of blood around her head. "She's been murdered!"

Lily floated above the body. "I can't sense her spirit. She must have passed to the other side already. Not everyone becomes a ghost, you know. Only those of us with unfinished business stay. I had a *lot* of unfinished business. There was—"

"Okay, we'll talk about that later." I felt a stab of panic. *Not again.* Another murder, and I'd discovered it. O'Malley had only just informed me that I wasn't a suspect in Larry's – and here I was standing over another body within a week. He was bound to be suspicious.

Suddenly, Lady Camilla popped out of nowhere. "Did someone say murder?" She looked down at Debbie's dead body. "Oh dear, yes, definitely murder."

The other ghosts materialised, and their chatter about the discovery filled my head.

"Quiet, everyone!" I shouted.

Their chatter stopped and they all looked at me.

"Thank you." I took a deep breath. For a split second, I considered walking out and making an anonymous call to the police – or simply leaving this mess for someone else to find. But that would be a cowardly thing to do. Besides, if someone had seen me arrive, then leave, and subsequently found Debbie's body, it would be even worse.

No, I had to call them. But instead of dialling 999, I stepped outside and called O'Malley.

He answered after one ring. "Ah, Trinity. To what do I owe the pleasure?"

"You need to get to Debbie's," I told him. "I came to call on her, and she's been murdered."

Ten minutes later, O'Malley arrived with a uniformed officer. "You sure know how to make a phone call memorable," he said, with a rueful smile.

"She's in the living room." I pointed. "I-I left as soon as I realised, so as not to mess up the forensic evidence."

He nodded and put his hand on my arm in a reassuring way. "Are you all right?"

My heart was racing. I was a nervous wreck. "Not really."

"Did you call an ambulance?"

"No, I— Should I have done? She's dead. There's nothing a paramedic can do for her now."

"It's a matter of procedure. We need medics to declare someone dead." He turned to the uniformed officer with him. "Call an ambulance. Trinity, wait here. More officers will arrive soon." Then he went inside and the officer followed him.

What had I been thinking of, going to visit Debbie? If I'd kept my nose out, I wouldn't be standing outside her home now, a potential murder suspect again. They'd want to take a statement, of course. That would take ages.

Then an icy chill ran through me. *Some killers pretend they found the body.* Maybe they'd think I'd done that.

A wave of panic rushed over me. Maybe it was the shock of seeing Debbie lying dead, or the months of getting the tearoom ready, only to be thwarted, or the stress of my marriage breakup and relocation. Everything rained down on me and I began to cry.

"That's a good idea," said Lily, putting a virtual arm around me. "Get all the emotion out. It's not every day you see a dead body, and you've seen two in just over a week."

"I'm sorry." I couldn't hold back the tears now.

I heard a sound inside the house and tried to stop. I always thought it embarrassing to be seen crying, and the last person I wanted to see it was DI O'Malley.

Phone held to his ear, he came out. "Bring CSI and a few other officers," he said. "Okay, bye." He ended the call. "Hey, are you all right?" He took hold of my shoulders as I sobbed. There was a moment where I thought he might hug me, but he remained the consummate professional.

"She was murdered?" I asked. "There was loads of blood."

"Yes, it's murder."

"Poor Debbie. First her husband, and now her."

"Indeed," said Lady Camilla, watching us. "Tears might endear you to the policeman. He seems a caring man."

He delved into a pocket and offered me a packet of tissues. I took one and dabbed my eyes. "I'm sorry. I should go home, but I guess you'll want a statement from me."

He nodded. "I'll get PC Coles to go with you and take the statement when you get home."

"Thank you."

"He's good at listening, just like me." Then he added as a joke, "But less handsome."

CHAPTER 25

A few hours later, my statement given, with many reminders and prompts from Lily as to what had happened, I sat nursing a cup of tea in front of the TV. I wasn't watching it; it was on to provide some company and background noise. None of the ghosts were with me. They'd all disappeared when I asked for some time alone.

I couldn't believe that Debbie was dead. It was only a few hours since I'd seen her in the street, fighting with Susan, and the day before she had visited my tearoom with Clive—

Susan. She certainly had a motive to murder Debbie.

I was staring at the TV screen, trying to shake off the shock of two people being murdered within a week, when I was roused by someone knocking at the door.

When I opened it, DI O'Malley was standing there. He looked tired. "Can I come in?"

I nodded.

He sat in the same place as he had a few days earlier. "I wanted to see if you were all right."

"That's very thoughtful. I'm just shocked. Poor Debbie. How did she die?"

"We'll have to wait for the autopsy to be absolutely sure, but it was most likely a blow to the head."

"That's horrible."

O'Malley nodded.

In the corner of my eye, I saw Mr Wickers appear. "Oh, it's the policeman again. I'll let Lily know; she likes to watch you two together. She's convinced you're meant for each other."

I was dying to reply, but O'Malley would think I was mad.

O'Malley cleared his throat. "So, I heard that you witnessed the fight earlier today between Debbie and Susan Mason."

"Yes, I was there."

"Can you tell me what happened?" His voice was soft.

"I was in Holly's craft shop. Kate came in and told us something was happening outside, so we went to see. Debbie and Susan were shouting at each other – well, no, Debbie was shouting at Susan – and they started fighting. Well, as much as two women can fight. There was a lot of hair-pulling and scratching."

"What were they fighting about?"

I looked away, then back. His eyebrows lifted slightly, encouraging me. "Debbie found out that Susan had had a brief affair with Larry."

"Interesting."

"You hadn't heard about that?"

"No. Do you know how Debbie found out?"

"Susan accused me of telling her."

"Now why would she think that?" There was a note of accusation in his voice.

"She told me about it in the tearoom. I didn't tell anyone, though."

O'Malley mused, "Maybe someone overheard her telling you."

I thought back to the day when Susan had confided in me.

As far as I could remember, only the ghosts had been near. But it seemed a few other people in town knew about it, including Holly and Heather. "That might be the case. But there's a lot of gossip going around town at the moment. Maybe someone else knew."

We sat in silence for a moment.

"Ask him if he wants tea," Lily said. "You should have asked when he arrived."

I shifted in my chair. "I'm sorry, I haven't offered you tea or coffee."

Lily gave a satisfied nod.

"Not for me, I should get going. Lots to do." I waited for him to stand up and take his leave, but he didn't. He stayed sitting there, looking at me with that hypnotic gaze. I felt myself going into a light trance.

Hastily, I filled the silence. "So, er, have you done a murder investigation before?"

"Plenty of times, when I worked in Belfast. I thought I'd left all that behind when I moved to Devon. I didn't think there'd be any murders here. I was hoping for sheep and cream teas, not corpses."

Before I could delve further into his past, the doorbell rang. "Excuse me." I got up and opened the front door.

Aunt Ruby stood on the doormat, holding a pet carrier. "Hello, darling," she said, kissing me on the cheek. "Do you have a minute?" She went straight past me, then stopped in the lounge doorway. "Oh! Hello, DI O'Malley. I hope you haven't come to arrest my niece." She put the pet carrier down.

O'Malley stood up. "No, not at all."

"Who's in there?" I peeped inside the carrier.

"The reason why I'm here," Aunt Ruby stated. "This is a stray cat found last week, dumped in a field near Tipton St John. I need you to look after him, just for a few days."

"Wait – no!" I stepped away from the carrier.

"Please, Trin," Aunt Ruby begged. "He's ever so sweet and friendly and no trouble at all. You'll hardly know he's here."

O'Malley bent down to look in the carrier. "He looks cute. What a nice thing to do, fostering animals that need a second chance."

"Er, well…" I tried and failed to think of a way to get out of it. "I thought you and the other animal-sanctuary volunteers had lots of people who could foster cats."

"We do, but they've all got too many cats now to take on any more. Honestly, if only people would get their cats neutered and spayed. Besides, this one needs to be on his own. He loves humans, but he hates other cats."

"No. No way. I haven't got any cat things. No bed, no litter tray, no food and no bowls."

Aunt Ruby waved a dismissive hand. "Don't worry, I've got all that in the car. All you have to do is give him a roof over his head and a bit of love."

"What about the cattery on the edge of town?"

"They're full. Come on, Trin. It's just for a few days, and you'd be doing me a huge favour."

I sighed. I had enough on my plate at the moment, what with my tearoom, a pack of demanding Regency ghosts and two murders. I scanned Aunt Ruby's expectant face and looked at O'Malley, who was clearly also waiting for my answer.

"Just for a few days," I found myself saying.

Aunt Ruby clapped her hands. "Thank you, darling! I'll fetch his gear, and then we can get him settled in."

O'Malley motioned to the front door which Aunt Ruby was hurrying through. "Better get going myself. Good luck with the cat. They're more unpredictable than suspects." And he followed Aunt Ruby out.

Aunt Ruby came back with an armful of cat paraphernalia

and arranged it all. I entered the hall to find a litter tray. In the kitchen there was now a mat with a bowl of water, and Aunt Ruby was putting packets of cat food on the counter.

When she had finished, she went to the carrier. "Right, young man, welcome to your new home." She undid the clasps of the carrier and lifted the cover.

The cat was a short-haired Russian blue. He looked up, a little surprised to find himself free. He jumped over the edge of the carrier and approached the settee.

"Oh my, he's gorgeous," I cooed. I sat on the floor next to him and he let me stroke him. "He's in good condition, too."

"That's because he's had TLC at the vet's for a few days."

"I bet that was expensive."

"It was, but that's why we raise all the money at the shelter, to spend it on the cats."

The cat rubbed his cheek on my hand and flopped on the floor, raising a paw to let me stroke his tummy.

"You're so cute!" I cooed.

"He doesn't have a name at the moment," said Aunt Ruby. "Perhaps you'd like to name him? At least, until he finds a permanent home."

I liked that idea. "Hmm, let's see." My mind ran through a list of names and one leapt out at me. "What about Wentworth?"

"What? That's ridiculous! Honestly, it's a stupid name for a cat. Does everything have to relate to Jane Austen?"

I raised my eyebrows. "If he's staying here, I can call him what I like. When he goes to his permanent home, they can rename him." I'd had a cat before, but it had been a few years since Noodles had died of old age, and I'd never thought of getting another. Cats were a tie, but having Wentworth here, knowing he would be at home, waiting for me at the end of the day, made me feel happy.

Aunt Ruby sniffed. "Wentworth it is, then."

I picked up Wentworth and held him close. "You poor

fellow. I'll look after you." He felt thin, but I'd soon fatten him up. I'd give him lots of treats.

"Right, then," said Aunt Ruby, interrupting my thoughts. "He needs feeding twice a day; the food is here. I'll come over with more in a few days and see how you're getting on. We won't put him up for adoption yet. And obviously, don't let him out."

"Okay." I'd thought Wentworth would struggle in my arms, but he seemed happy to be held.

Aunt Ruby stroked him. "There now, young man. You look after Trinity for me."

When Aunt Ruby left, I felt a weird vibration in my body. Lady Camilla and Lily appeared and bent to examine Wentworth, who looked up at them and meowed.

Lady Camilla put her nose in the air. "I never liked cats. Useful for catching mice, but not much else."

Lily clapped her hands. "He's gorgeous. I wish I could stroke him." Wentworth flopped on the floor again, showing her his tummy.

"I think he can see you!" I said.

Lady Camilla floated to the other side of the room. "Some animals can. Usually it's dogs. Although there was that lion that saw me when— No, I mustn't talk about the other ring-owners. Anyway, the lion saw me and tried to pounce. It gave me such a shock. And the lion, too, when it saw it hadn't got me."

I laughed.

"It's no laughing matter, my dear. I was frightened half to death. If I hadn't already been dead, it certainly would have killed me."

Wentworth stood up, looked at Lady Camilla and meowed.

"He can definitely see you," I said.

"That's delightful. I love it when cats can see me." Lily floated over to Wentworth and pretend-stroked his head.

I picked him up again. "Well, Wentworth, you're going to fit right in."

That night, Wentworth slept on my bed, and I woke to find him curled against me. He purred contentedly as I stroked him. If I'd been a cat, I would have been purring, too.

CHAPTER 26

The next day, word had got out that the tearoom was open again, and a steady stream of locals and tourists meant we were kept fully occupied. The ghosts were enjoying the busy tearoom and promised they would listen to all the customers' conversations for anything that might help solve the murders.

There was a lull in the afternoon, but it wasn't until there was just one table of customers left that the ghosts came to the kitchen to report back.

Lady Camilla cleared her throat, and I looked up from loading the dishwasher. "We have heard something that you need to know."

I straightened up. "What is it?"

"Mr Wickers overheard two women talking earlier. They said Clive wasn't out of town on the day of the murder."

I froze. "Mr Wickers heard that?"

He floated towards me. "I did."

I gave a hollow laugh. "Nice try, but I'm not falling for that again." I continued to load the dishwasher.

Mr Wickers lifted his chin. "I'm not joking this time. I really heard it. Two, ahem, rather rotund ladies, Anne and

Maria, were talking about helping at the charity shop for donkeys, whatever that is. Anne swore blind that she saw Clive pass the shop on the day of the murder."

"Anne and Maria?" I knew them: ladies in their sixties who formed part of the backbone of Sidmouth society. They volunteered anywhere and everywhere they were needed: fairs, charity nights, committees, amateur dramatics… If there was something going on in Sidmouth, they were involved.

"I'm sure that's what they called each other. The one with short curly hair kept talking about how she wanted her husband, Ken, to go to London for work."

I nodded. That was definitely Anne. It was well known that she volunteered mostly to get away from her husband.

I stared at Mr Wickers. I wanted to believe him, but I couldn't. "Look, I'm prepared to put your previous joke behind us, but doing it again isn't nice."

"I'm not! If you know Anne, visit her and she will confirm what I said."

I considered. The worst-case scenario was that I'd be caught out again and make a fool of myself in front of Anne. However, if Mr Wickers was right, this would move the case along. If Clive wasn't away, he had no alibi. And if he had no alibi, he could be the murderer.

"What about Victor, Larry's cousin?" I said. "He arrived in town a few days ago. The word is that he stands to inherit money from Larry, then suddenly Debbie ends up dead."

"Why would he murder Debbie, though? He was already going to inherit money from Larry," Mr Wickers countered.

He had a point. "All right. I'll speak to Anne. But if you're lying again, I'll take the ring off and leave it at home for a month."

Locating Anne was easy. She volunteered weekdays at the Donkey Rescue charity shop in the middle of the high street.

I entered the shop, and after a brief look around, located Anne by the till.

I grabbed the nearest thing to buy, a red woolly hat. Not exactly needed at the moment with the mild weather lately, but it would do. "Hello, Anne, how are you?"

I placed the hat on the counter.

Anne was sitting on a stool, untangling a bunch of knotted chain necklaces. She looked up when I spoke. "Oh, hi, love. I'm all right, thanks. We loved your tearoom."

"Thanks. It was good to see you in there."

"What can I do for you today? This hat?"

"Well…" I looked around the shop. There was only one customer at the back. "I heard you saw Clive walk past the shop on the day of Larry's murder. Is that right?"

Anne put the chains down and moved her glasses onto the top of her head. "I think it was that day. You see, we'd had a delivery from a house clearance at Newton Poppleford. A lady had passed away, and her family didn't want most of her stuff. Not a surprise, really, as most of it wasn't sellable. Very tatty. Mike had to do a tip run in the end. It's a good job we get a discount from the council, otherwise we couldn't afford it."

She glanced at the chains, then continued. "Anyway, Mike came with the delivery about eleven. I remember, because I'd had my break fifteen minutes before, and I still had my cup of tea. I was telling Mike where to put everything out back, and that's when I saw Clive. At least, I think it was Clive. He was in the Roxburgh car park, getting something out of his boot. I don't know him to talk to, but I recognised him. I've seen him around Sidmouth with Larry a few times, and at the garden centre. I love going for a browse at weekends, don't you?"

"So was it on the day of the murder, or not?" I tried not to sound impatient.

"I'll check. Hold on, let me look at the inventory…" She opened a drawer behind the till, pulled out a scruffy note-book and leafed through it. "Ah, yes, here it is…" Her finger tapped the page. "Yep, definitely the day of the murder.

Thursday, wasn't it? Oh, hang on. Mike did a delivery the next day, too, so I'm not sure. It might have been Thursday when I saw him, but it could have been Friday."

I tried to contain my growing frustration. "So you can't remember which day you saw him?"

Anne pursed her lips. "I'm sorry, my lovely, I can't."

I sighed. "Well, thanks for trying."

I paid for the hat, then walked to the door.

"We'll be back in the tearoom soon," Anne called after me. "We loved it."

"See, I told you the truth." Mr Wickers wore a wounded expression as soon as we were outside in the street.

"So you were telling the truth this time, Mr Wickers, but can you blame me? You have form."

He looked puzzled. "Form?" He patted himself. "I don't have a form any more. I'm a ghost."

"Having form means that you have a reputation. You've tricked me before, so now I'm suspicious of you."

"I see."

"What do I do now? Clive could have been in Sidmouth on Thursday or Friday. If it was Thursday, he could have come to the tearoom and murdered Larry when everyone thought he was away."

"Surely someone would have seen him, and the police would have scrutinised his alibi?" said Mr Darby.

I nodded. "Anne must have been mistaken. She can't even remember what day she saw him. And no one mentioned seeing him in the tearoom."

"Still…" Mr Darby considered. "I think you should find out for sure which day it was."

I raised my eyebrows. "How, exactly?"

"Go to his office and look for clues."

I winced. "You mean sneak into his office and look for evidence of him being away?"

"Yes. There should be something in his diary."

I put my hand on my hip. "I'm not breaking into his office."

Mr Darby gave me a rare smile. "You wouldn't be breaking in. Not if you went when the garden centre is open."

"No. No way."

But later on, the thought that Clive might have been lying and could be the murderer, wouldn't leave me alone. So much so, that I resolved to go to the garden centre the next morning and find out.

CHAPTER 27

Bloomhaven Garden Centre was on the outskirts of the northern side of town. Everyone knew it, because everyone went there on sunny bank holidays to look around, have a drink in the café and buy plants they didn't need.

I'd never been green-fingered. In London, our garden had been the size of a postage stamp, and a few years before we divorced, Dean had laid artificial grass. I hated it, but it had served a purpose: to keep the garden as maintenance-free as possible. Both of us worked long hours; neither of us had time to garden in the evenings and at weekends we were too exhausted.

I parked and walked past pallets of compost, bags of decorative gravel and trays of seasonal plants, to the entrance. The place was busy with people coming and going.

Just inside, I heard the trickling of numerous water features. I sighed. This was heaven. The thought of buying an indoor water feature for the tearoom crossed my mind, but I dismissed it when I read the price tags.

The aisles were stocked with indoor plants, garden tools, insecticides and fertilisers. To the left was the café, and to the right, a small craft section, selling greeting cards and fresh-cut flowers. To the rear was the outdoor plant section.

I browsed for a while, the ghosts following me and commenting on the place. But to get into Clive's office, I had to locate it first.

I moved to an empty aisle full of artificial flowers, and murmured, "I need you to find Clive's office."

Mr Darby nodded and disappeared through a wall.

A minute later, he returned. "Go to the greeting-card section, and you will see a door marked *Staff*. The office is through there at the end, and it is empty. I have checked his wall calendar, but it is blank on the day of the murder. You will need to look on the computer."

"Thanks."

I found the right section and the staff door. There didn't seem to be any sort of lock. I pretended to look at something on a shelf nearby, waiting for the area to clear. Other customers moved on, but no one went in or out of the door. I glanced around. The two checkouts were busy, with growing lines of customers.

I swallowed my fear, pushed the door open and slipped through.

On the other side was a long corridor with four doors. The first on the left had a toilet sign, and the next had a small window. I peered in. It looked like the staffroom. On the other side was a storeroom and at the end, an office.

"It's the door at the end," Mr Darby prompted.

I tried the door and it opened. I slipped inside, closing the door behind me.

Clive's office was small. Two desks took up most of the room: a large one covered in papers, with a computer, and a smaller one at a right angle. I guessed this belonged to a secretary or assistant.

On the wall behind the smaller desk was a year planner. I took out my phone and snapped a picture, then looked for the date of the murder. There was nothing on that day, just as Mr Darby had said. Then I looked more closely and realised the planner showed the staff holiday schedule.

"I'll look through his papers," said Mr Darby, and dived into the desk. A moment later, the top of his head poked out.

"Anything?" I whispered.

Mr Darby frowned. "Patience, please. These things take time."

I moved closer to the desk. The computer was switched off. As my finger moved towards the power button, I heard voices outside: one male, one female.

My heart almost stopped. I swallowed nervously. There was no time to hide…

The door opened.

CHAPTER 28

Clive saw me and stopped dead. "Trinity. What a surprise. What on earth are you doing in my office?"

"Oh, hello, Mr Hayward. One of your staff said you were in your office and gave me directions. But you weren't here, obviously. I've only just come in." I hoped I wasn't blushing.

His eyes narrowed. "I was dealing with an issue on the other side of the building." He squeezed past me and sat at his desk. I could see Mr Darby's head sticking out of it. "What can I do for you?"

Mr Darby floated out of the desk. "Tell him you're here because you're interested in buying some plants for the tearoom."

"I'm interested in buying plants for my tearoom," I repeated. "You know, to add some greenery. I was also thinking about an indoor water feature." This visit would cost me.

He smiled. "Ah, what a lovely idea. We have an extensive range of high-quality indoor plants. Most of our water features are outdoor ones, but we can order in any you like from the indoor range. There are brochures outside."

"Lovely."

"You didn't need to come and talk to me about it, though. One of my staff could have helped you."

Mr Darby hovered above Clive's shoulder. "Ask for a discount."

"I wondered if you offered a discount for local businesses. I always have an eye for a bargain."

"A shrewd businesswoman," said Clive. "That's commendable. I'll instruct my staff to offer a ten per cent discount."

"Ask him for fifteen," said Mr Darby.

"Could you manage fifteen per cent?" I echoed.

"Twelve and a half, and that's as far as I can go."

"Done." I was going to hold out my hand, then thought better of it.

"Well, when you've picked out what you want, let the staff know."

"I will."

"Bye, then, Miss Bishop."

He turned to his computer and switched it on. I saw myself out.

In the shop, I browsed the plants, which were strong and healthy but ridiculously expensive. However, it gave my heart rate time to return to normal and allowed my panic to subside.

"You can thank me later for getting you out of that pickle," said Mr Darby, floating next to me.

"Thank you," I whispered under my breath.

"It's a good job I was there, because you would never have thought of that. You looked completely startled. As startled as Miss Elizabeth, when she first read my letter of explanation."

"That's because I was. Where were the others? They should have warned me that Clive was coming." Then his words sank in. "What do you mean, your letter of explanation to Miss Elizabeth?"

Mr Darby lifted his chin. "The others thought I should help you on my own because…" He paused dramatically. "Because they said we needed to bond."

I suppressed a laugh. "Bond? Us? Well, you have been moody and distant most of the time."

Mr Darby sighed. "It's hard for me. Every time there is a new ring-holder, I need time to adjust."

"Don't like change, huh?" I felt a wave of compassion for him. Then I thought about Mr Darcy in *Pride and Prejudice*. He was a lonely figure, only fully opening up to people when he knew them well. Jane Austen seemed to have captured Mr Darby's character splendidly in her novel. "Anyway, you didn't answer my question about Miss Elizabeth. Who is she? What was the letter?"

Mr Darby cleared his throat. "Shouldn't we depart?"

I looked towards the exit. "I'm leaving now."

"Oh, but what about the plants for the tearoom?"

"I'll leave that for now. Anyway, did you find the diary?"

"I almost forgot about that in all the excitement. I found the diary, but there was nothing in it for the day of the murder or the days before. If Clive went away on business, he didn't put it in his diary. Make of that what you will."

CHAPTER 29

The next morning, I opened the tearoom on time and a steady stream of customers came in. During a lull, Aunt Ruby visited and cornered me as I was putting together orders in the kitchen. "I can't stop for long, but I thought I'd see how... how Wentworth's doing," she said, standing in the doorway and scanning the customers for anyone she knew.

"I left him curled up in his new bed, snoring. His food was all gone, so I imagine he was sleeping off his enormous meal."

"Lovely!"

"He's been no trouble at all. He even curls up on the bed with me at night." He really wasn't any hassle and I enjoyed playing with him. He loved chasing the feather on a stick and particularly enjoyed his catnip-filled mouse.

"It sounds as though you like having him around."

"I do, but I'm not getting too attached. I just hope his forever home is good enough for him. Have you found someone yet?"

Aunt Ruby smiled. "Possibly."

"Well, let me know when you do."

"What else have you been up to?"

"I visited Anne in the charity shop and asked her about seeing Clive on the day of the murder. I was trying to find out if Clive's alibi for the day of the murder was true. Anne thought she might have seen him near the shop. On the day of the first murder, I mean. There was nothing in his diary to say that he was away."

"How do you know that?"

I lowered my voice. "I sneaked into his office and had a look." That was technically untrue, but there was no way I could tell my aunt about Mr Darby.

"Oh, good girl!" Aunt Ruby had a glint in her eye. "Did you get caught?"

"Nearly."

Mr Darby appeared, wearing an aggrieved expression. "I am wounded that you didn't mention me. You're like all the others. No one ever tells a soul about me. It's as if I don't exist."

I gave him a hard stare. I'd speak to him properly later.

"Clive wasn't at the tearoom, though," I told Aunt Ruby. "So why would he lie about being away?"

"Maybe he sneaked in, murdered Larry, then sneaked out again," Aunt Ruby replied.

"But someone would have seen him."

"True. The most likely answer is that he's having an affair."

"That's very cynical."

"Darling, when you get to my age, you'll be as cynical about men as I am." I hoped not, but I didn't say it out loud.

"Knock knock!" said a familiar voice from the open back door, and my cousin Francis stepped in. He took his police cap off, sighed and sat on the bar stool placed to the side.

"My darling boy, how are you?" asked Aunt Ruby.

"Mum! Don't call me that outside the house!"

"Cup of tea?" I asked, before they came to blows.

Francis rubbed the back of his neck. "Don't mind if I do. I popped in to see how you're getting on. I've been pretty busy lately; two murders have kept us all busy."

"I'll leave you two to it. See you later, Francis." Aunt Ruby kissed me on the cheek, gave Francis a look that said *at least she doesn't mind my attentions* and left via the tearoom.

I prepared Francis a tray with scones, clotted cream, jam and a pot of tea at the same time as the other orders. "Ooh, lovely. I'm starving." He tucked in, and I sat down next to him in the tearoom. Lady Camilla floated over and tutted at Francis's table manners.

"So, Francis, do you have any news about the murders?" I asked. "Or are they still keeping you in the dark?"

Francis sipped his tea, then put the cup down. "Not with Debbie's case. As it didn't happen in your tearoom, they're less strict, but I think it's mainly because we're short-staffed at the moment. They think Debbie must have known who killed her because she let them in. However, I was sent to knock on all the nearby residents' doors and question them, and no one was seen going in or out of Debbie's place for hours before the murder would have happened, so they didn't come in that way. Debbie's kitchen has a back door which leads to a small patio area, and that can be accessed from a back street via a hidden path. So we're back to square one."

"There must be CCTV, though, or one of those doorbells with cameras? Even if it is at the back of the street." I felt hope ebb away.

"That would have been very convenient, but no." He took another bite of scone.

"Has O'Malley questioned anyone?"

"Susan, of course. After their street fight, she was the

prime suspect, but she was let go. Her alibi must have checked out, whatever it was. Then there's David, but the B&B owner said he didn't leave his room all day."

"Does O'Malley think the same person killed them both?"

Francis ate the last bite of scone and nodded, his mouth full.

"That makes sense," said Lady Camilla, who had floated in and was listening. I was getting so used to the ghosts being around that I'd started to forget they were ghosts. "Husband and wife, so the police need to check who will inherit from them."

I gave a discreet nod to Lady Camilla, then repeated what she'd said to Francis.

"O'Malley's onto it," he said. "He's trying to locate the will but he hasn't found it yet. Not everyone has one, anyway."

"What's he like to work with?" I asked.

Francis's expression transformed to a bright smile. "His accent's divine, don't you think? When he asks you to do something, he looks at you directly and he asks so nicely that it's impossible to say no. He has a sort of hypnotic look in his eye."

"Yes, it's strange, isn't it?" I recalled the various times I had fallen under O'Malley's spell. It would be very hard to say no to him. "What happens if Larry and Debbie didn't have a will?"

"Everything goes to the closest relative. Not that they had much. They weren't poor, but they weren't rolling in money, either, despite the investment in the garden centre. They didn't have much else."

"Sounds like money probably wasn't the motive, then. What about forensic evidence?"

"Still waiting on it. Nothing stood out, apparently." Francis drained his cup. "I'd best be off. Duty calls. Thanks for the scones." He stood up and left.

I turned to Lady Camilla. "What next?"

She shrugged. "I would ask that handsome detective."

I smiled. Seeing O'Malley again would never be a chore. But would he think I was interfering in the case if I questioned him?

CHAPTER 30

When it was time for my break, I went into the street outside the tearoom to get some fresh air and phone O'Malley. There were still plenty of people milling around and my Regency outfit got a few strange looks. I walked away from the seafront, not really sure where to go, but I needed to clear my head. The ghosts followed, looking around. They seemed easily amused when out and about.

I passed the Ship Inn, one of the oldest pubs in town and distinctive with its white stone exterior and thatched roof. I did a double-take when I saw Larry's cousin Victor sitting by the window. He was facing a young, smartly dressed man.

I walked past, then stopped at the next shop and looked in the window, trying to decide what to do.

"What's in here?" Lady Camilla said, eyeing the shop's display.

"I need one of you to go into the pub and listen to what Victor and the man with him are saying. They're by the window."

A couple of tourists walking past, smiled at me, seeming not to mind that I was apparently talking to myself.

"Eavesdrop?" said Mr Wickers. "Oh, goody! I volunteer." He bowed, then floated into the pub.

I turned to the other ghosts. "Mr Darby, will you go, too? I still don't trust him completely."

Mr Darby bowed, then followed Mr Wickers into the pub.

I stood by the shop window, wondering how far from the pub I could go before it pulled Mr Wickers and Mr Darby away. I should have brought flyers for the tearoom to hand out.

After ten minutes, I sent Lily in to see what was going on. She returned after a few minutes. "The two men are talking about Victor's police interview. The other man asked Victor where he was when Debbie was killed. Victor's most upset that he's a suspect."

The two men left the pub, with Mr Wickers and Mr Darby right behind them. They shook hands and with a final word, parted. Victor went towards the seafront and the other man went straight past me in the opposite direction.

"So?" I asked the two ghosts, as soon as the men were out of earshot.

"The other man was a lawyer," said Mr Wickers. "They were discussing his police interview yesterday. He was most upset to be asked to provide an alibi for Debbie's murder."

Lady Camilla sniffed. "Providing an alibi is nothing to be upset about – if you have done nothing wrong."

"What else were they discussing?"

"The likelihood that Victor will remain a suspect because his alibi is weak," said Mr Darby.

"Yes," said Mr Wickers. "It seems that he was in his hotel room for most of the day when Debbie was murdered."

"Doesn't the hotel have CCTV?" I asked.

"Apparently not," Mr Wickers said. "That's why he was nervous. He said he has to leave tomorrow."

"That does sound suspicious. Did they mention anything else?"

Mr Darby bowed. "That is all we are able to report, madam."

"In that case, I need you to go into his hotel room and look around," I said. "Perhaps something in there might indicate a motive."

Mr Wickers grinned. "Excellent. More snooping!"

I marched towards the Royal Hotel with the ghosts following me and stood outside it. "Go into reception, find out what room Victor's in, then look around it."

The ghosts looked at each other. "We could check every room," Mr Collingwood said.

Lily giggled. "I would love to snoop around every room!"

Lady Camilla tutted. "I refuse to snoop. How vulgar!"

I sighed. "Look, decide between yourselves what to do, but you need to find Victor's room and see if there's anything in it that might implicate him."

All the ghosts except Lady Camilla disappeared.

Five minutes later, Lily floated down from one of the hotel windows above where I was standing. "We found his room and the men are looking through his things, but there's a nasty ghost in the hotel. He doesn't like us being there, and he's causing trouble." She shivered. "I don't like him. You have to come."

"Me?" I said. "What can I do?"

"He's much older than us, and he has dreadful manners. He told us to get lost, and he's pushing us and trying to shove us out." Lily looked genuinely distressed.

"Lady Camilla, surely you could go and make him see sense?" I said. Maybe she could channel some Lady Catherine de Bourgh energy.

Lady Camilla sniffed. "I don't like confrontation. Trinity, you had better go."

"Do you think I'll be able to see him, because of my ring?"

"Possibly. Some of the other ring-owners could see other ghosts, but not all."

Lily nodded. "It depends on whether the ghost wants to be seen, really." She looked up at the windows. "Quick, there's a real stink going on up there. I can hear them fighting."

I followed Lily into the hotel, past the deserted reception, up the stairs and into a long corridor. Lily floated ahead of me. It was deathly silent.

"Are you sure about this?" I asked, pausing for a moment.

"Shh." She put her finger to her lips. "How strange! There was a real hullabaloo a moment ago, and now it's silent."

"Maybe it's all over."

It wasn't over.

Mr Darby came through the wall backwards. His throat was gripped by a masculine hand, the owner of which was still behind the wall.

He saw me and Lily. "Sorry about this," he managed to splutter. "The hotel ghost doesn't appear to like visitors."

"Bit strange, seeing as he lives in a hotel," Lily stated.

Mr Darby made a sort of gurgling sound. "I meant ghostly visitors."

The arm came through the wall, followed by a ghost dressed in Tudor-era finery, with an embroidered doublet and breeches that ended just below the knee. His leather boots had seen better days. His face was framed by a well-groomed Van Dyke beard. He glanced at me and Lily, then let go of Mr Darby, who clutched at his neck and then straightened his cravat.

"Hello," I said.

"Can you see me?" the Tudor ghost asked.

"Yes, I can."

"Verily, 'tis an age since such events last transpired. Methinks it was the year of our Lord, 1956." He made a graceful, courtly bow from the waist and a sweeping motion with his arm. "Good morrow, fair lady. I find myself most fortunate to make thy acquaintance. I am Sir Reginald Ravenscroft, erstwhile resident of this establishment. And to whom do I owe the pleasure?"

That name was a bit of a tongue-twister. I curtseyed. "A pleasure to make your acquaintance, sir. I am Mistress Trinity Bishop. I have come with my friends to…" I paused, reluctant to admit that I was snooping. "We are investigating a most heinous crime and have come to this establishment in search of a particular suspect."

"Ah, verily! Most curious, mistress. A mortal, in companionship with ghostly beings! You are unusually attired for a modern lady." He eyed my Regency gown.

"Oh, I, er, I like dressing up. Pray, sir, why are you averse to our presence?"

Sir Reginald stood upright. "I find no pleasure in the company of other ghosts within mine own establishment. 'Tis most disquieting."

"Then I pray you will forgive this intrusion, kind sir," I said. "We shall spend only a short time in your establishment, and then we shall leave."

Sir Reginald studied me and considered. "Indeed, I have never been capable of denying a gentlewoman aught that she doth request."

Then he turned to Mr Darby. "Verily, good sir. I do beseech thy pardon for mine prior conduct. I knew not thou wert here in service to a lady, and one so fair and youthful, at that."

Mr Darby pursed his lips. "A gentleman should always accept an apology from another gentleman." I could tell, although he spoke the words, he didn't want to.

"What precisely dost thou seek, mistress?" asked Sir Reginald.

I was about to open my mouth when one of the bedroom doors opened, and an elderly couple came out. "Hello," I said, and smiled at them, hoping they wouldn't ask what I was doing hanging around the corridor dressed in a Regency costume.

They smiled at me, then walked past and out by the door to the stairs, watched by the ghosts. The moment they had gone, I said, "We need to find the room of a man named Victor. We are looking into a murder."

"Murder!" Sir Reginald shouted. "By golly, I *will* help you! Await me here, mistress." And he disappeared through the wall.

"Why don't you follow him?" I asked Mr Darby.

"I shall *not* be following him," he replied, with a huff.

Mr Collingwood volunteered in his place and vanished through the wall.

A few minutes later, Mr Collingwood and Sir Reginald reported their findings. "We've found him and been through his room, and we can report he is probably not the murderer," said Mr Collingwood. "We found a receipt for flowers which he sent to Debbie in condolence, and a card torn up in the wastepaper basket. In it, from what we could piece together, he'd written a lengthy message explaining that he wanted to help her in this difficult time and he thought that Larry would have wanted him to look out for her."

I sighed. "That doesn't sound like something a killer would do. Unless it's an elaborate bluff."

The rest of the ghosts muttered and nodded.

I turned to Sir Reginald. "Thank you, kind sir, for your help. I will for ever be your grateful servant."

Sir Reginald made another flamboyant bow. "It is I who shall be your servant, mistress."

I headed for the tearoom. I'd already been away much longer than I should have. "Thank you, everyone," I told the ghosts. "Your help is much appreciated."

By the time I got back to the tearoom, ready to help Emma and Carol, I realised I'd completely forgotten to phone O'Malley.

CHAPTER 31

After a long day, I finally found myself back home, with my feet up on the sofa and a cup of tea. Despite serving it to my customers all day, I didn't think I'd ever get tired of drinking it myself.

I settled down to watch TV and was flicking through the channels when I noticed Wentworth pawing and hissing at something by the bookshelf.

"What are you up to?" I asked him. Wentworth didn't respond, so I got up and went over for a closer look.

Wentworth was concentrating so hard on staring at whatever it was that he didn't even notice me. It took a moment for me to see what he was stalking: a tiny mouse darting between the books. It moved so quickly that I could hardly get a look, but then it disappeared into the spine of a book.

I closed my eyes for a moment and shook my head. Had I really just seen a mouse move through a solid object? Was it… Could it be…

"A ghost mouse?" I said out loud, with a laugh.

I pressed the turquoise stone of the ring. Within moments, Lily and Mr Wickers materialised in the living room.

"Can animals be ghosts?" I asked.

Lily floated over to me and looked at Wentworth. "Yes. Sometimes. Not many, though. And this cat certainly isn't."

Mr Wickers' eyes narrowed. "Why are you kneeling and looking at the bookcase? Are you trying to get us back for that joke about the Jane Austen expert? I'm ready for you, you know."

"It's not a joke. I'm sure I saw a mouse disappear into a book, and Wentworth saw it, too."

"A mouse, you say?" Mr Wickers adjusted his cravat and scanned the bookshelf.

Lily laughed and clapped her hands. "Oh, how delightful – a mouse that even a cat can't catch!"

Wentworth's head moved, then he lifted himself onto his hind legs and pawed at a book. The ghost mouse made a dash across the room, followed by Wentworth, and vanished into the wall.

Mr Wickers sighed. "We should probably do something about it."

"We need to guide it to the other side," Lily said. "Even mouse souls deserve peace."

"How?" I asked, genuinely curious.

Lily and Mr Wickers exchanged glances, then focused their attention on the spot where the mouse had disappeared. They started to murmur words which sounded like incantations. Then they stretched out their hands, and the room filled with a strange, ethereal light.

I heard a squeak. The ghost mouse came back through the wall, glowing with a gentle light. A glowing white hole materialised in front of it and it floated in. Then the hole closed, and the room returned to normal. The whole thing had taken seconds.

Wentworth had watched the whole thing and remained puzzled as he looked around for the mouse.

"Thank you," I said. "Who would have thought my evening would include helping a ghost mouse to find its peace? I have a question, though. If you can help animals to reach the afterlife, why don't you help each other, too?"

Mr Wickers shook his head. "We've tried. It doesn't work for humans."

"That's annoying," I said.

"Indeed." Lily and Mr Wickers dematerialised, leaving me alone with Wentworth.

I returned to the sofa, picked up my cup of tea and took a sip. Life with ghosts was never dull.

"Come on, Wentworth. Come and sit with me." I patted the empty seat next to me, beckoning him.

He jumped up, settled beside me and started to purr.

CHAPTER 32

The next morning, at home, Lily floated through the dining room wall and hovered in front of me. I was sitting at the table with my laptop. "What are you doing?" she asked.

"I'm looking at the Sidmouth Business Consortium's financial reports."

"That sounds boring."

"Knowing about money is a modern-day necessity. Boring, yes, but it's also handy to know bookkeeping. It helps me run my tearoom."

"Why are you looking at someone else's financial reports?"

"I wanted to see what was going on there. I wasn't looking for anything in particular, but something doesn't sit quite right."

"What's that?"

I turned the laptop around and pointed to the screen. "Every year, for the last four years, there's been a big payment for training. I wondered what it was, so I looked through the minutes and discovered it was for Heather to gain a qualification in accountancy and auditing."

"And?"

"I looked into it. The course only takes two years, even part-time. I need to go to the consortium's office to see if there are any other documents about it there. It's open every day from nine to ten am."

Lily grinned. "I can help."

"You mean like Mr Darcy at Clive's office?"

"Exactly."

I closed the laptop and got ready to go out. Ten minutes later, I was outside the consortium's office.

Lily floated behind me, and nearly went through me when I stopped at the door. The sign said that the office was open, so I went in.

"Hello!" Heather was sitting behind her desk, dressed quite casually in black leggings and a mustard-coloured top. On the other side of the desk was a man in his fifties, who glanced at me. I scanned the office and saw a large metal filing cabinet in the far corner. That would be where I needed to search.

"Hi, Heather," I replied.

"I'll be with you shortly," said Heather. "I'm just finishing with Nigel."

"Shall I wait in the hallway?"

"Please."

I went back out. "You need to look in that cabinet," I told Lily.

Lily floated into the filing cabinet. Then her head reappeared. "What exactly am I looking for?"

"I can't tell you here!" I said.

Heather and Nigel stopped talking and stared through the doorway. I felt myself blushing. I needed to find a better way to talk to the ghosts in public. Sign language wouldn't work either. Maybe I'd just have to leave the ring at home sometimes.

Then I had an idea. I took out my phone and held it to my ear.

"Oh yes!" cried Lily. "What a good idea. You can whisper. I can still hear you."

"Can you read the documents inside?" I murmured.

"Yes, I can. It takes a bit of getting used to, but I can even read a book or a newspaper."

"That must mean that you've read a lot of things."

"You wouldn't believe it. Over the years I've read anything and everything. Can't get on with ebooks, though. I can't turn the pages."

"I love reading when I'm not busy. Always have, always will, even with dyslexia. I mean, TV is all very well, but there's nothing like a book."

"That's why I like you," Lily said. "Anyway, what am I looking for?"

I thought for a moment. "I'm not sure. But anything about bank accounts, payments or training could be useful."

Lily disappeared again. I kept my phone to my ear as though I were still on a call. "I've been meaning to ask you," I said. "You can see other ghosts…"

"Yes."

"Have you met any other famous writers? I mean dead ones."

"A few… but they were boring and we didn't get on. I won't name names."

"Spoilsport. I know; look for anything to do with a company called 'GTFCC': invoices, receipts or anything like that."

"Right." Lily disappeared, and I took my phone away from my ear.

Nigel said goodbye to Heather and she saw him to the door. "Sorry about that," she said, once Nigel had left. "How can I help you?"

"Oh, er…" I tried desperately to think of something. "I-I'm just here to find out when the next meeting is."

Heather gave me a tight smile. "It's tomorrow night, at the Blue Ball Pub."

"Thanks!"

"Is that all?" Her eyes narrowed. "I'm sure you're on the email list. Let me check." She moved back to her desk.

Lily floated out of the cabinet. "I've found it!"

"What?" I whispered.

"You said to look for anything about money and training. Well, I've found four invoices from a company called GTFCC. The invoices are all for eight thousand pounds and they come once a year. Distract Heather, and I'll lift them out of the cabinet."

"You can move things?"

"Yes. I'll have to generate wind to do it, but I just need to concentrate." Lily floated back into the filing cabinet.

"What a lovely vase," I remarked, and walked over to Heather's desk for a closer look. I faked a stumble and knocked a vase with flowers over. It tumbled onto the floor, shattering into several pieces.

"Oh my God, I'm so sorry!" I exclaimed.

Heather frowned. "It's okay, accidents happen." She got up, went to a cupboard and pulled out a dustpan and brush. "I'll clean it up."

"No, let me," I insisted. "It was my fault, after all. It wasn't valuable, was it?"

As I stooped to clean up the shattered vase, Heather turned to get some paper towels from a shelf. That was the moment Lily had been waiting for. She floated some papers out of the filing cabinet and slid them into a business booklet, one of a stack on a nearby coffee table.

"I think I've got all the pieces," I said, standing up and handing the dustpan to Heather.

"Thank you, Trinity. Just leave them there; I'll take care of it." Heather's tone was clipped: she was still focused on the mess.

"All right, if you're sure. I should head back," I said, moving towards the door. As I passed by the coffee table, I picked up the first booklet and checked the papers were safely inside.

"See you tomorrow night," Heather said, as I made my way to the door.

"Absolutely," I replied, gripping the booklet tightly. "Again, I'm really sorry about the vase."

Once I had left the office, I sighed with relief. Hidden in an innocent booklet, I had documents which could hold the key to everything. Lily floated after me, a triumphant look on her face.

I walked slowly to the tearoom, searching for GTFCC Training on my mobile phone. I found no mention of the company on the internet. By the time I reached the tearoom, I'd discovered that GTFCC Training wasn't on the *Companies House* website either.

"I'm starting to think it doesn't exist," I told Lily.

"What doesn't exist?"

I jumped. In front of me was O'Malley. "Er, hello, how are you?"

O'Malley smiled. "Very well, thank you. What's so interesting that you aren't looking where you're going?" He leaned over to look at my phone.

"Nothing." I clicked the side button and the screen went black.

"You're hiding something," he said, with a smile. His Irish accent was more pronounced than usual.

I blushed. "Nothing important."

"You wouldn't be looking into one of the suspects, would you?"

Lily floated between us. "I think he's flirting with you.

Maybe he thinks you're on one of those matchmaking sites on the phone."

"How do you know about those?" I said, and instantly regretted it.

O'Malley looked confused. "So you are looking into a suspect?"

"I'm just searching for something. That isn't against the law, is it?" The words came out more bluntly than I'd intended.

"No." He looked nonplussed.

Lily stared at O'Malley, then waved a hand in front of his face but he didn't react.

"Sorry," I said. "I didn't mean to sound so grumpy. Did you want to speak to me?"

"No, I was just walking this way. The pavements are very narrow here in Sidmouth. There's barely enough room for one person, never mind two."

"You get used to it, and it's only this part that's so narrow. The rest of the town has larger pavements."

"Well, goodbye for now. Watch your step – literally!" He stepped into the road to walk round me.

"Bye."

He smiled at me over his shoulder.

"That didn't go very well," Lily scolded. "Next time you see him, you must be extra nice. Remember, a woman should show more interest than she feels in order to encourage a man."

I gave Lily a look. "Have you been reading *Pride and Prejudice* lately? That's exactly what Charlotte Lucas says to Lizzy about Jane and Bingley."

"She came up with that one herself, but after all this time, it's still true."

I wasn't sure that was a good idea. I'd never been a flirty woman.

"But, Lily, isn't it a bit... dishonest? To lead someone on like that?"

Lily fluttered around me. "It's not dishonesty; it's strategy. And sometimes, the heart needs a little push in the right direction."

I considered her words. "I suppose a bit of encouragement couldn't hurt. But if I'm going to do this, it'll be in my own way."

"A touch of sincerity with a sprinkle of charm. You'll see, he won't stand a chance."

CHAPTER 33

That evening, I looked over the papers. It was clear that Heather had been up to no good. But if I was going to confront Heather about her embezzlement, it had to be done in public. There was no way Heather would admit it in private. My best opportunity would be at the consortium meeting, in the function room of the Blue Ball Pub the following day. Hopefully that wouldn't be too late.

When I arrived, about ten people were already there, chatting to each other. I poured myself a cup of tea from the urn and scanned the room. Heather was there, chatting with a woman and looking relaxed and happy. That was about to change.

I'd made the decision to wear the magical ring. I felt I needed the ghosts for moral support, and they were keen to witness some drama.

Edward Whitaker, the mayor, was sitting at the head of the table. He coughed to get everyone's attention. "Good evening, ladies and gentlemen. I'd like to welcome you to this evening's consortium meeting. Before we start, we must pay our respects to Larry and Debbie Cunningham, who were sadly taken from this world last week, and especially Larry, who served this town as chairman of the consortium. There will now be a minute silence in memory of them."

That surprised me. All the members, including Heather, had hated Larry. But I supposed they had to do the decent thing and act as if they were genuinely sorry.

When the long minute was over, Edward Whitaker surveyed the room with a smile. "Right, let's get started. First, are there any apologies for absence?"

"None," said Heather. "Everyone's here."

"In that case, we can move to the second item on the agenda."

My pulse was racing. Did I dare to speak up and reveal what I knew? If Heather was the murderer, I didn't want to be her next victim. That said, I hadn't actually discovered anything to suggest that Heather was the murderer. But maybe Larry had…

I stood up. "I have something to say."

"Er, hello, Miss Bishop," said Edward. "It's nice to see you here, but we rarely stray from the agenda this early in the meeting. Can it wait until 'any other business'?"

"No, it can't wait. It's urgent."

Edward cleared his throat. "In that case, go ahead."

All eyes were on me. I took a deep breath and composed myself before speaking. "As you know, Larry was murdered in my tearoom. However, that's not why I'm here. Or not exactly. I was looking at the SBC's finances, and I found something of interest. Each year, for the last four years, the SBC has paid thousands of pounds for Heather to attend accountancy and audit training. I looked into the company providing the training, GTFCC Training Limited, and found that it didn't exist. Well, it does, but it's owned by Heather and her husband. She's been paying her own company to train her."

You could have heard a pin drop.

"Furthermore, I have evidence that Heather mocked up a

company letterhead with a fake address and opened a different bank account."

Heather stared at me in horror.

"It was easy to find," I said. "I'm surprised your auditors didn't find it. You do have auditors, don't you? Or does Heather do your auditing?"

The members looked at each other. Edward turned to me. "Miss Bishop, are you accusing Heather of stealing money from the consortium?"

"Well…" I considered. "Yes, I suppose I am."

A murmur of disapproval went round the table. Heather sat stony-faced.

"You can't come into a public meeting and make an accusation like that," Edward said.

"Why not, if it's true? I wouldn't accuse her if I didn't have proof. And while I can't say for sure what she's done with the money, her last week of 'training', six months ago, coincided with the Annual World Poker Championships in Las Vegas. Heather's a big fan of poker. Aren't you, Heather?"

Heather stood up, then sat down again. All eyes were on her. "How dare you!" she spluttered.

I delved into my bag and took out some photocopies of the documents Lily had taken from the cabinet. I passed a set to Heather, who stared at them. "How did you get these?" she asked.

Then she sighed. "All right, I admit it. I took the money. It wasn't for a training session; it was for a trip to Vegas. And boy, did I need it." She looked around the table. "Working with you all sucks the life out of me. I do everything. *Everything*. I needed something to look forward to so that I could cope with the stress."

A murmur of disapproval went round the table and a stern-looking woman in her late fifties folded her hands over her chest. "This is preposterous!"

A tall man of about seventy stood up. "We can't simply stand by and accept this!" he bellowed.

I sat down, wide-eyed. I hadn't expected Heather to admit her guilt so easily.

Lady Camilla gave a satisfied nod and the other ghosts applauded. "Well done, Trinity."

Heather gathered her papers and her bag and made a beeline for the door. No one stopped her leaving.

I thought about following Heather, but I'd done what I needed to. Now it was up to the members to deal with Heather – and potentially, the police.

CHAPTER 34

The next morning, my mind was still full of what had happened at the consortium meeting. None of the consortium members had contacted me as yet, but I supposed that first the committee would have to decide what to do.

I was walking to the tearoom when I saw Susan ahead of me, walking in the same direction. Where was she off to this early?

I hadn't spoken to Susan since her fight with Debbie in the town square. Part of me wondered why O'Malley hadn't arrested her, because surely she was the prime suspect in Debbie's murder. A fight in the middle of the street over an affair was definitely a motive, if ever I saw one. Whatever alibi she'd given, I'd be checking it over with a fine-tooth comb.

I picked up my pace and was getting close when Susan turned right towards Blackmore Gardens, past the gym, then into the library. I followed her, and if I were honest with myself, I wasn't sure why. I found her browsing the fiction section.

I approached Susan with a friendly smile, inhaling the

familiar scent of old books that always seemed to fill libraries. "Looking for anything in particular?" I asked.

Susan looked up and her demeanour changed. She wasn't pleased to see me. "Trinity. No, just looking for something with a bit of romance. I could do with some in my life right now."

"Are you a fan of Jane Austen?" I asked, attempting to establish a connection through my own love of literature.

Susan scanned the books on the shelves. "Sort of. I mean, I've read a couple of them. I prefer the TV or film adaptations."

I was surprised Susan hadn't mentioned the brawl with Debbie or the fact that Debbie was dead. Then again, we were having a friendly chat.

"Er, so how are you?" I inquired.

Susan glanced at me, then continued to browse. "Me? Fine, thanks."

"I mean, after the – altercation the other day, and the fact that Debbie is dead."

Susan stared at me. Then she sighed, her shoulders visibly sagging. "I'm fine. It was quite traumatic being attacked like that by Debbie. She was wild, which is pretty ironic, considering that she was having an affair herself."

"What?" Did I hear her correctly?

"Oh, yes. With Clive. They'd been at it for months, if not longer."

"How do you know?"

Susan laughed. "There are no secrets in this town. Every Wednesday night when Larry was at the consortium meeting, he'd sneak into her house."

"I had no idea. Well, anyway, I just wanted to check in and see how you are. It must be a very stressful time for you."

"It is. The police asked me all sorts of questions about where I was on the day Debbie was murdered. As I told them,

I was at work, with lots of witnesses. Not that I got much done."

So that was why O'Malley hadn't arrested her. Her alibi was airtight.

But if Susan didn't kill Debbie, who did? Who would want both husband and wife dead? The murders had to be connected. They hadn't been killed by chance.

I left the library and sat on a bench in Blackmore Gardens. The ghosts sat with me.

"None of this makes sense," I complained. "Susan has an alibi, and Victor didn't do it either. Honestly, this case is very annoying."

Lady Camilla nodded. "It is indeed. I'm still not sure about David. He is very suspicious, if you ask me."

"But O'Malley hasn't arrested him."

"Well, that might just be because he hasn't found the evidence yet. Why don't you try and expose David? Tell him that one of those camera things shows him returning to the tearoom. If it's true, he'll admit it. If it's false, he'll deny it."

"He might deny it anyway."

"I'll wager that if he thinks there's video evidence, he'll have no choice but to admit it."

I sat, thinking. "I suppose the worst that could happen is he'll be angry with me, but in any case, I'll never see him again. He's leaving the area soon."

CHAPTER 35

I decided not to call on David at his B&B again. I'd learnt from Meg, the B&B owner, that David went for an early-morning walk along the beach and up Jacob's Ladder to the cliff top, finishing at Connaught Gardens. There, he would have coffee at the café, then return to the B&B. I mused on the advantages of the business owners' grapevine. They certainly kept their eye on everyone. They probably kept their eye on me, too, but I decided not to think about that.

I took up my position at the top of Jacob's Ladder, a series of wooden steps leading up a steep cliff at the southern end of the seafront. At the top of the steps was a garden and a café, and the ladder itself was part of a longer footpath along the coast.

David came huffing and puffing up the steps at five past nine. He mopped his red face with a handkerchief and walked towards the café.

"Hello!" I stepped forwards, blocking his path. "How are you?"

It took David a moment to respond. "Er, hello. You, again."

"Out on a morning walk? Me, too, before I open the tearoom."

"Yes. I like to walk along the seafront. I'm making the most of it before I go home."

"Fancy a coffee?"

He paused for a moment, then nodded.

We sat on one of the benches outside the café, looking out over the cliffs. There was hardly a cloud in the sky. A small fishing boat moved past, and we watched it for a while.

"I didn't think I missed Sidmouth when I moved to London twenty years ago," I said. "Now that I'm back, though, I don't think I'll ever leave."

David gave me a wry smile. "It's a strange person who wouldn't enjoy living by the sea, but we can't all do it."

"No, I suppose not."

David took a sip from his coffee cup. "Look, I'm sorry for being so rude the other day. I was still getting over being interrogated for hours about the murder."

"Why don't you tell me about what happened with Larry."

He leaned back against the bench. "I told you what he did. He groomed my daughter."

"What happened?"

"We had a business together, back in the day: a building services yard. It stocked quality building materials and made a lot of money. We were friends, too. When we weren't working together, we were playing golf or having dinner. This was when my girls were growing up. I have two daughters, Caitlin and Josie."

"Larry doesn't have children. Is that right?"

"That's right. He always said he didn't want any, and Debbie went along with it."

"So what went wrong between you?"

"He had his eye on Caitlin. Unknown to me, he'd been showering her with compliments, and he persuaded her to meet him on the quiet. They started a relationship. It was only when Debbie caught them that the whole thing came out."

"How old was Caitlin?"

"Eighteen. Larry was fifty-eight."

I winced. That, while legal, was totally inappropriate. I'd met Dean at the same age, but he'd been eighteen, too. A summer romance, which had turned into a move to London.

"I can tell from your expression how you feel about that," said David.

"Any parent would feel the same, I'm sure."

"You'd hope so. Caitlin was devastated when I told her to break it off. She told me that she loved Larry, and he would leave Debbie for her. She couldn't accept that any of it was wrong. Then I found out that Larry had been paying attention to Caitlin since she was fourteen. Fourteen! What he did was disgusting, but what could I do? There was another way to get at Larry, though. I threatened to go public with what he had done unless he left the area and never came back."

"I'm not sure I would have been so calm about it," I said. "What made you wait all this time to confront him?"

"I wasn't calm at the time. When I told him to leave the area, he sold me his share of the business and disappeared. That's when he moved here."

"And five years later, he contacted Caitlin on social media."

David nodded. "She's married now, to a husband the same age. The last thing she needs is a reminder of the stupid mistake she made five years ago. I came here to tell him to back off."

"No wonder you were angry."

There was a long pause as they looked out to sea.

"I didn't kill him," said David. "I told you that before. I wanted to, but I'd never do it. I'm not sorry he's dead, I'll admit it, and I won't mourn him. Debbie, now… that was wrong. Debbie never hurt a fly, poor woman. Larry controlled her, and I've heard that he had more than one affair."

David shook his head. "I've no idea what women found so appealing in him. It's not as if he was good-looking."

"He was always horrible to me," I replied. "But I've heard that when he wanted to, he could be very charming. And lots of women are lonely. Look, David, I believe you when you say you didn't kill Larry. But someone says they saw you round the back of the tearoom just before Larry was killed."

That made David sit up. "Who?"

"Someone from one of the other shops. You came back, didn't you?"

He sighed. "Yes. I wanted to speak to him again. To tell him that if he tried it again, I'd make sure everyone in Sidmouth found out what he did. I sneaked in through the back door in the kitchen, then out through the garden. It was in the middle of the opening ceremony; you were giving your speech. But when I entered the garden, Larry was already dead. I knew that if I sounded the alarm, I'd be accused, so I left as quickly as I could. The police examined me and found none of Larry's blood on me or my clothes. As I said, when I came back, he was already dead."

"I believe you," I said.

"I appreciate that. There's no reason why you should, given what I've just told you. Will the witness go to the police?"

I bit my lip. "There is no witness, David. I made that up to get to the truth."

David looked at me for a long moment, then exhaled slowly. "You know, for a second there, I was angry. But I can see why you did it. You needed to be sure."

"I did. I'm sorry for lying, but I wanted to hear it from you."

He nodded. "I should be annoyed at you, but for some reason I'm not."

"Sometimes you have to bend the rules to get to the truth," I said, trying to lighten the mood.

"So, what now? Are you going to tell that detective I went back to the tearoom?"

I considered this. I didn't want to hide anything from O'Malley. "I think you should tell him," I said. "But I need to find out who really killed Larry and Debbie. And bring them to justice."

"I'll think about it," David said.

CHAPTER 36

That evening, after a busy day at the tearoom with the customers and the ghosts, I went for a walk, first along the seafront, passing the shelter where I'd sat with O'Malley, then back through the town to Blackmore Gardens.

I was halfway through the small gardens when I saw a short woman in her sixties, dressed in black leggings and an oversized green jumper, with a Scottie dog on a lead. It was Lorna, a woman I knew a little from Holly's Craft Emporium classes. We'd attended a five-week course on crochet and chatted a few times. Lorna had picked up crochet quickly and made excellent progress. I'd struggled, and decided by the end that I didn't have the patience or skill to go much beyond the basics. Lorna had always been a few minutes late for class, though – why? Then I remembered: she'd come straight from her job as an evening cleaner at Bloomhaven Garden Centre.

I went over. "Hello, how are you?"

"Oh, hello. I'm all right, thank you. Just taking Freddie out for his evening walk." Freddie sniffed my feet and jumped up, begging for attention.

"I bet you can smell my cat!" I laughed, patting Freddie. "Are you still working in the garden centre?"

"Yes, but I finished early tonight."

"That's good. What's it like, working for Clive?"

Freddie pulled on his lead, trying to reach a tree. Lorna allowed herself to be tugged along and I followed. "He's all right," said Lorna. "Doesn't really notice me, to be honest. Most people don't notice women over fifty, especially not cleaners."

I made a note of this information in case it was ever useful in future. "Has anything changed at the garden centre now that Larry is dead? He was an investor, wasn't he?" I didn't wait for Lorna to answer. "Did he go to the centre much?"

"Not much. Usually only when he and Clive wanted to argue. He'd always come after closing, when I was working. Such rows they had." She shook her head. "They had a massive one about a week before Larry was murdered."

"Really? What about?"

Lorna paused, weighing me up. "You've got to promise not to say anything. I rely on that job. If Clive found out I was talking about him, he'd sack me."

"I'm the soul of discretion," I said, trying not to show my excitement at fresh information.

"Larry wanted to pull out as an investor and sell his shares."

"Why was that a problem?"

"Clive couldn't afford to buy him out. They'd been planning to buy another garden centre near Exmouth, with a loan guaranteed by both their homes, but Larry said it was too risky and he wanted out. Between you and me, I think it was really because they didn't get on, and Larry had had enough. Although, everyone knew Clive and Debbie were having an affair."

Everyone except me. "Did you ever see them together?"

"No, but Claire's friend Margaret saw them in Seaton at the beach café. The one at the end of the esplanade."

"That doesn't mean they were having an affair, though."

Lorna gave me a look that said *Don't be naïve*.

I nodded. "Okay, so they were having an affair. You don't sneak off to another town for coffee for no reason."

"Very indiscreet. Honestly, though, if I were married to Larry, I'd have an affair, too. Horrible man."

"So they were rowing a week before Larry was murdered and Larry wanted to leave the business. Do you think it might have been because he'd found out about the affair?"

"Possibly. I only heard part of the row, and they'd been at it for a while then. Larry stormed out a few minutes later with a face like thunder."

"Well, it's a shame they were fighting, but I guess that's what happens in business. Partnerships break up." I was glad I had sole ownership of my business.

"Clive came out afterwards and stomped about. I needed to clean his office, and I had to knock on his door to get him out. He apologised for the row, left the office and went home. Strange thing is, when I started cleaning, I noticed a mobile phone on the desk. I went out to give it to Clive and called to him, but when he turned round, he was on his phone already. I thought that meant it must be Larry's phone, but Clive said it was his."

"Two mobile phones?"

"One for business and one for personal, I think."

My mind was whirling. Two mobiles? It could be nothing, but then again… "Well, how interesting. And don't worry, mum's the word. Just shows, you can't trust anyone these days, even if you're married."

"Too right. I gave up on men years ago." Freddie pulled on the lead again, dragging Lorna away. "See you soon."

My mind was full of what I'd heard. Larry and Clive rowed about the garden centre, and perhaps Larry had found out about Debbie's affair with Clive. My instinct was to call O'Malley and find out what he knew, but I'd promised Lorna that I wouldn't say anything, and anyway, it wasn't a crime to have two mobile phones. There were plenty of perfectly good reasons why someone might have more than one. Clive had been out of town when Larry was murdered – O'Malley had checked – but what if he'd taken his other phone and it wasn't registered to him? A burner phone, they called it. Would it matter if he was definitely out of town?

I wasn't sure what to do, so I went home to discuss it with the ghosts.

CHAPTER 37

I sat on the sofa in my living room, the ghosts gathered around me.

"I think it's highly suspicious," Lady Camilla said, in a stern tone. "Two of those phone devices? Why would you need two? And they were seen out together. Terrible behaviour."

Mr Collingwood nodded reverently. "Adultery is one of the seven deadly sins. Matrimony is a holy and serious undertaking. The vows a man and woman make should be taken seriously, however long ago the marriage took place."

"Which is why I never married," Mr Wickers said, with a wink.

"What do you think I should do?" I asked. "I promised Lorna I wouldn't say anything, so if I tell O'Malley, she'll know it was me."

"He might already know," Mr Wickers said.

"He might. But what if he doesn't?"

"Speak to O'Malley," said Mr Darby. "Ask him what evidence they have that Clive was out of town on the day of the murder. You don't have to mention Lorna or what she said."

"Good idea, I'll phone him." I picked up my phone and dialled his number.

He picked up straight away, and I put the phone on speaker so the ghosts could hear. "Hello, Trinity," he said pleasantly. His Irish accent sounded stronger on the phone. "What can I do for you?"

That was straight to the point. "Er, hi. I know it's late, but I have a strange question for you."

"Go on."

"How did you check Clive's alibi?"

I heard him sigh. "Look, you know I can't talk to you about the case."

"All right, so how about I ask you a general question? If you were checking out someone's alibi, how would you do that?"

After a pause, he spoke. "We check the place they went to and speak to people who saw them."

"Is that all? You don't check their mobile phone data? It tracks them, doesn't it?"

"It does, although it's not always helpful. That data shows their phone was somewhere, but that doesn't always mean they were with the phone."

"But it helps."

"Yes."

"So, if, for example, you were checking someone's alibi, would you always check their mobile data?"

"In serious cases like murder, yes. We always do that."

It was my turn to pause. "Okay, thanks," I said, eventually.

"Look, we've checked Clive out fully. Which is why we haven't arrested him."

"So you'll know he has two mobile phones?" I asked quickly.

"What? No. He has two? How do you know?"

"I can't say. But trust me, he has two. Isn't that suspicious?"

"Not necessarily. Lots of people have a work phone and a home phone, especially if they need to separate them. Many companies will give employees a phone as well as the SIM as part of the work package. Seeing as you can only have one number per SIM here, no-one wants to be swapping SIMs over all the time."

I sighed. "You're right. I'm sorry for phoning so late. Bye."

"Bye, Trinity."

I ended the call. The ghosts sat looking at each other.

I sighed. "So they did use mobile phone evidence for Clive. But if he has two phones, he could have taken his phone, left it somewhere to make people think he was there, then retrieved it later."

Lady Camilla pursed her lips. "It sounds rather contrived. And a lot of effort."

"Not if he'd planned it. It would be worth it for the alibi."

A text message pinged on my phone. It was from my son, Oliver.

Hi Mum, hope the tearoom is going ok. Miss you. O.

Lily hovered over the phone. "Your son is checking up on you. How nice."

Mr Darby nodded. "A noble thing for a son to do."

I replied:

Miss you too Ollie, hope you can come down and visit soon. xx

"Where does your son live?" Lily asked.

"In London, with his dad. He's just started university."

Lady Camilla made an approving noise. "That is excellent. What is he reading?"

"Computing," I replied. "I don't understand any of it, but he's a whizz."

"Back in our day, there was law, theology, philosophy, literature, history and languages," said Mr Darby.

"What did you study?" I asked.

"I read history at Oxford."

"A noble subject to learn. I love history. If I wasn't dyslexic, I would love to have gone to university."

"There are means to study remotely," he replied. "You can use that computer to learn."

I smiled. "Get you! A ghost from at least two hundred years ago teaching me what I can do over the internet."

There was a glimmer of a smile on Mr Darby's face. "I've learnt a great deal over the years."

"I can see that." I yawned. "I think it's about time I went to bed."

The ghosts dematerialised and I went upstairs.

———

The next day, I couldn't help thinking about what I'd learnt from Lorna about Clive's two phones. If I could get hold of one, I might be able to find out whether he did use it just for work.

I checked the clock. It was nearly closing time for the garden centre. I needed to look around Clive's office again. If I got caught, I could always say that I was looking for Lorna. Yes, that would be my excuse this time.

I closed the tearoom dead on five, got changed quickly, then made my way home, got in the car and drove to the garden centre. At five thirty I pulled up in the almost deserted car park. When I entered, the café was closed and its staff had gone. In the main shopping area, one or two customers browsed. In the outside section were rows of plants, but no customers.

I approached the door to the staff area. When I was sure no one was looking, I opened it and went straight to Clive's office.

"Go inside and see if it's empty," I said to the ghosts.

Mr Darby floated through the wall, then reappeared. "The office is empty."

I slipped inside.

I glanced around Clive's dimly lit office. It hadn't been this dark and eerie the last time I was there.

I went to his desk and searched the drawers. The first two had typical office supplies: pens, notepads, a calculator. But in the third drawer, I found what I was looking for. Hidden under a stack of documents was a mobile phone.

I touched the screen and it asked for a passcode. "I should have thought of that. There's no way I can get into it."

Lily loomed over my shoulder. "Try his birth year."

"I don't know when that is, and it might take some time to find out."

"Try 1234," Mr Wickers said.

I looked doubtful but tried anyway. It didn't work.

Mr Collingwood shot through the door, and I nearly jumped out of my skin. "I wish you'd stop doing that!" I scolded.

He bowed. "My sincerest apologies, madam, but Clive is about to enter the room."

"What?" Oh no. Being caught twice in Clive's office would be too hard to explain.

I looked at the mobile phone in my hand. Should I take it? He might track it if I did. I opened the drawer to put it back, but before I could close it, the door opened and Clive walked in.

CHAPTER 38

"Miss Bishop. In my office again." He paused for a moment, then shut the door behind him. "What do we have here? Have you been going through my desk?"

I swallowed, hard. Clive didn't seem too surprised to find me there, and that was worrying. "Clive, you have a lot to explain."

He laughed. "You're trespassing in my office. I think you're the one who should explain."

I decided to go on the attack and confront him. "It's not that unusual for someone to have two mobile phones, but you hid the fact, you had the extra one, from the police."

"What? My mobile phones are none of your business. You're a presumptuous, nosey thing, aren't you?"

I stood my ground, refusing to be intimidated. "You can call it what you want, but I call it searching for the truth. The extra phone, Clive. It connects you to the crime scene, doesn't it?"

Clive's façade of amusement began to crumble.

"You've been watching too many detective shows, Miss

Bishop. That phone is for... business purposes only. Untraceable, for client confidentiality."

"But which clients?" I pressed, feeling the stakes rise with every word.

Clive's eyes narrowed. "You're out of your depth. This isn't a game. This isn't one of your little afternoon tea mysteries you can solve and be hailed as the town's hero. You need to watch yourself."

"And yet, here I am, uncovering your secrets," I retorted, my pulse quickening. "I've already informed the police. If anything happens to me, they know where to start looking."

Clive's laugh was devoid of humour this time. "You think you're clever, don't you? Meddling in affairs that are beyond you. Debbie and Larry... they were just the beginning."

"Why did you do it, Clive? Why did you kill Debbie and Larry?"

For a moment, the room was steeped in silence. Then Clive let out a sigh. "I wondered when you'd figure it out, snooping around," he said, his voice cold. "Debbie and Larry were obstacles, Trinity. They stood in the way of something much bigger, therefore they had to be removed. Larry wanted out of the business. He didn't want to expand. I saw its true potential. Saw a nationwide chain of glorious garden centres just like this one." His eyes glazed over as he imagined his empire.

A chill ran down my spine. I couldn't believe what I was hearing.

"So what would stop you from getting another investor instead of them?"

"He wanted to sell the business to get at his money. I tried to get another buyer, but no one was interested. He wouldn't give me more time."

I didn't know what to say to that.

"But why Debbie? Surely she would have kept the money in the business? Especially as you were having an affair."

A strange look came over Clive's face. It was only there for a moment, and I thought it might be regret. Then he drew himself up and sighed. "Debbie. Dearest Debbie. She couldn't get over the fact I'd killed Larry. A true Lady Macbeth. Consumed with guilt."

"Lady Macbeth? Did she tell you to kill Larry?"

"What? No. It was my idea, but she knew. She saw me enter by the kitchen and go out into the garden. She knew it was me." He sighed again. "Unfortunately, she couldn't live with the knowledge. It was only a matter of time before she blabbed."

Clive moved a step closer, his eyes locked on mine. "They were the obstacle; now you've become an obstacle, too."

As Clive stepped closer, my head pounded and my hands trembled. My knees felt as if they would buckle beneath me. I needed to run, but how could I get past Clive? I was as tall as him, but he was wider and stronger. I was trapped.

"I need your help," I cried to the ghosts.

Clive smiled an evil smile, thinking I was talking to him. "The only way I'll help you, Trinity Bishop, is in helping you to depart this world."

"Quick!" Lady Camilla commanded. "Lily!"

Lily waved her arms, and the papers on Clive's desk rose into the air. Mr Collingwood pointed to the office lights, which flickered, then brightened.

Clive looked up at the lights. "What the—"

"Pretend you're doing it," said Lily.

I pointed to the lights, then waved my hands like Lily. The ghosts continued to make the papers fly and the lights flicker.

Clive frowned. "What are you, some kind of witch?"

"Yes," I said, with a grin.

"I'm going to darken the room," said Lady Camilla. "Wave your arms again, and when it's dark, make your escape."

I did as she asked and it went black.

"What the— You *are* a witch!" cried Clive.

I pushed him into the table. "I'll get you!" he shouted.

I scrambled for the door, my heart thumping, but couldn't find it. I felt along the wall, then finally found it, turned the handle and was out of the room. I ran for the staff door, Clive staggering after me.

I sprinted across the main shopping area to the entrance, but the large glass automatic doors were shut.

"You should have taken the fire exit," Clive panted. He had caught up with me and was standing a few feet away.

He took a step forward.

The ghosts were standing around him, gazing at me.

"We can't lose the new ring-owner now," Lady Camilla said sternly. "I'm just starting to like her."

Clive walked slowly towards me. "I shall enjoy this," he said, grinning.

"Lily, start your wind again," Lady Camilla commanded.

Lily waved her hands and the wind picked up.

"Faster!" ordered Lady Camilla.

Mr Collingwood pointed to the lights and they flickered.

Clive looked up at the lights, his hair streaming in the wind. "Witch!" he snarled.

Lily groaned as she focused the wind on Clive. It increased, until he looked as if he were in a wind tunnel. He struggled to stay upright.

"Run!" shouted Mr Darby, and pointed to the nearest fire exit. I ran around a pyramid of weedkiller, through the indoor plant section, then pushed the bar on the door and stumbled into the car park.

CHAPTER 39

t took a moment for me to get my bearings. I was in the loading area. There were pallets of garden supplies everywhere: bags of gravel, compost, slabs and plants.

The ghosts came into view as though they were being pulled towards me. If Lily wasn't blowing a gale on Clive, he'd appear any moment.

I looked around the car park and spotted my car just a few yards away. I rummaged around in my pocket for my keys, ran towards it and pressed the button to unlock the doors.

"Clive is over there!" Mr Darby shouted.

I saw him coming out of the front door. He stopped when he saw me. "You witch!" he shouted.

I was about to pull open the door, when a black Ford Mondeo drove into the car park. DI O'Malley was at the wheel. "Thank God!" I cried, relief washing over me. He parked a few spaces away from me.

Clive walked backwards towards the garden centre doors. Our eyes met for a moment, then he turned and ran inside.

I ran to the passenger side of O'Malley's car and pulled the door open. "Clive's the killer, and he just tried to kill me, too!"

O'Malley got out, a concerned look on his face. He put his hand on my arm. "Was that him running inside just now?"

"Yes."

"You stay here. I'll call for backup and try to find him."

"What? You can't go in there alone! He's a double murderer!"

"I know how to handle myself. Don't worry. I'll be fine." He took out his phone, tapped the screen and held it to his ear, then he ran to the front door. This time, it opened. O'Malley disappeared, and I stood still, panic going through me. What if he was killed?

Mr Darby floated over to me. "You must go in and help him. We'll find Clive, but you need to get closer."

I stared at him. "I don't want to go back in! Why couldn't O'Malley just wait?"

I couldn't believe it. Mr Darby wanted me to go back in. But he was right. O'Malley would find Clive much quicker with the ghosts' help.

As soon as I was inside the building, the ghosts went in search of Clive. I moved to the middle of the retail area to maximise where they could search.

I couldn't see O'Malley, and wondered if he'd gone into the staff section. Then I saw Mr Collingwood near the outside area, floating high up in the air. "He's in one of the sheds. O'Malley is out here, too, but he hasn't found him. Come and tell him, madam."

I followed Mr Collingwood to the outside area as fast as I could. There were rows of waist-high benches holding various plants, and beyond those, six sheds and three greenhouses. He pointed to the long greenhouse at the end. It was at least forty foot long. You could barely see inside because of the green algae on the glass.

I approached it and saw O'Malley peering inside.

"I thought I told you to stay in the car park?" he said, with a hint of annoyance.

"He's in that greenhouse at the end," I told him.

"You're sure? How do you know?"

I couldn't tell him that a ghost had told me. "Um, I'll tell you later."

He gave me a curt nod. "Stay here."

"Shouldn't you wait for backup? He might have a weapon."

He ignored me, went towards the greenhouse, then cautiously opened the door. "Clive, I know you're in there," he shouted.

There was no response.

The ghosts gathered around me. "Go inside," I told them.

"I thought you wanted me to stay outside," murmured O'Malley, staring into the greenhouse.

"Sorry, I was, um, talking to myself."

The ghosts went in.

"I'm coming in to talk to you, Clive," O'Malley said, and stepped inside.

I followed. The dimly lit greenhouse had a sunken pond in the middle which stretched almost the whole length of it. I could just see large koi carp in the clear water, moving near the surface as they waited for food. On each side of the pond and against the glass were plants blocking out the sunlight, casting shadows and giving the greenhouse an eerie atmosphere. Part way down was an area filled with sculptures and water features.

"She's a witch, you know," Clive said from the end of the greenhouse.

O'Malley glanced at me and I shrugged.

"He's hiding behind a big plant at the end," said Mr Darby.

"I think he's behind a big plant near the end," I whispered to O'Malley.

"You've got good eyesight."

I said nothing.

"I'm coming down, Clive, just to talk," he said.

"Keep the witch away from me," Clive replied.

We reached the end of the greenhouse and saw Clive cowering behind a plant. He looked up and saw us. "I said keep her away! She's a witch. She can do things…"

"No one's going to hurt you, Clive, but you need to come out of here."

"Get her away from me. She did things to me."

I flushed, though luckily O'Malley couldn't see. "I don't know what you mean, Clive," I said flatly.

"Liar! She tried to pull me into a tornado!"

O'Malley turned to me. "I think it might be best if you leave, Trinity. Clive's scared of you, and he won't come out if you're here."

"All right." I wanted to say something threatening to Clive but resisted.

I went outside, and the ghosts took it in turns to tell me what was happening.

"O'Malley's telling Clive that you've gone out and there's nothing to fear," Mr Wickers reported. "He's still refusing. What a coward."

Lily giggled. "I did nearly pull him into a tornado, though."

I blinked at her. "Remind me never to get on your bad side, Lily!"

I heard police sirens in the distance: help was on its way. I ran into the building, then out though the front door and greeted the three police cars that had just pulled into the car park. Then I directed them to the greenhouse. Within a few minutes, Clive was outside in handcuffs.

As O'Malley and the other officers talked, Clive kept looking at me, his face full of fear.

"He *is* scared of you," said Lady Camilla, with a satisfied nod.

"Good," I whispered. Clive had been planning to kill me here. It was his turn to be scared.

O'Malley finished directing a uniformed officer and came over to me. "Are you all right?"

I nodded, though I definitely didn't feel all right. If it hadn't been for the ghosts, I might be dead by now.

"Do you want to do the witness statement here, or at the station?" O'Malley asked.

I felt my knees tremble. "I'd rather go to the station."

CHAPTER 40

At the police station, I gave my statement to one of the PCs with Francis there as a support. The ghosts were there, too. Mostly, they were a silent, supportive presence, but they also reminded me of what had happened when I had trouble remembering.

I couldn't tell the police the full truth, of course. How could I say that several ghosts connected to the magical ring on my finger had helped me escape? So, instead, I said I pushed past Clive and made a run for it.

Once the statement had been taken, the PC left. O'Malley came in with another cup of tea and sat down. "I'm afraid it's nowhere near as good as the tea you serve, but it's warm and I put a sugar in. I thought you might need it."

I was grateful for his thoughtfulness. "So, have you interviewed Clive?"

"We're just waiting for his lawyer to arrive, then we will. He's ready to admit what he did, though. He said he didn't want you near him. He still says you're a witch." O'Malley gave a small laugh.

Our eyes met. "That term is used against women all the time," I replied. "Such a misogynistic thing to say."

O'Malley stared at me for a moment, his gaze hypnotic. "He kept rambling on that you could control the lights and the wind."

I shook my head and laughed. "Ridiculous. Imagine if I could do that! I wouldn't be running a tearoom, I'd be taking over the world!"

O'Malley smiled. "Well, all I can say is that you were very lucky to get away. Larry and Debbie weren't so fortunate. There's danger in going solo, you know: the police are here for a reason. Despite what some may think, most police officers are good guys who want to protect the public."

"Why did you suddenly turn up at the garden centre?" I picked up the tea and took a sip.

He sat back in his chair and shrugged. "Call it intuition, or a hunch. I couldn't stop thinking about what you said regarding the second phone, so I came to talk to Clive about it."

I nodded.

"Looks like your hunch was right, though." There was a note of humour in his voice. "That was good investigation. Ever thought about joining the police?"

I wasn't sure if he was being serious or not. "That's a hard pass from me," I said. "I'd much rather be my own boss."

O'Malley stood up. "Take your time and finish the tea. There's no need to rush home. I'll see you soon. I need to interview a double killer." He moved towards the door.

"Thanks," I replied. "I'm really glad you turned up when you did."

He nodded and left the room.

Lily giggled. "DI Handsome definitely fancies you."

———

The next day, in the tearoom, every table was filled with

customers. At least it kept me from thinking about everything that had happened the day before.

Mid-afternoon, Aunt Ruby came in. She arrived in a flurry, dressed in a vibrant skirt, an embroidered tunic, and layers of beaded necklaces. I was rushing around, taking orders, clearing dirty plates and looking after the customers.

Aunt Ruby finally cornered me in the kitchen as I loaded the dishwasher. "News in the town is that Clive has admitted to the murders," she said. "He'll appear at the magistrates court tomorrow morning."

"You mean Francis told you?"

Aunt Ruby gave a knowing smile. "You know Francis can't tell me anything that goes on in the station. It's against the rules."

I closed the dishwasher and switched it on.

Aunt Ruby leaned against the counter. "It's nice to see you busy here, Trinity, but it must have been terrible for you. I mean, what if he'd actually killed you?" She enveloped me in a brisk hug. "You're my dear niece."

"It's best not to dwell on these things." I opened a cupboard and took out a tray of scones.

"Hmm, well... you know what you need to take your mind off it?"

"I don't need anything."

"You do, and I have just the thing. Another cat to foster."

My heart sank. "Does that mean you've found a forever home for Wentworth?" I wasn't sure I wanted to part with him so soon. He hadn't been with me very long, and he was a reason for me to look forward to going home. The thought of parting with him made me sad. Besides, the ghosts liked him, too, and he could see them.

"What? No, not yet, but there are more cats that need fostering."

"I'm not sure my house is big enough, and you said he

didn't like other cats. Anyway, could I keep Wentworth? What do I have to do to adopt him?"

Aunt Ruby clapped her hands. "That's wonderful! Of course you can keep him. I was hoping you would. I'll get the adoption papers to you in the next couple of days."

Emma came into the kitchen. "Order for a Mrs Bennet, tea for two, table six."

I straightened up. "Right, better get on."

Aunt Ruby gave me another hug. "You've made my day, dear. Now, go on, those teas won't serve themselves. And don't worry about Wentworth. He's found his forever home with you." With a cheerful wave, she headed out of the kitchen, leaving me smiling and ready to tackle the rest of the day.

CHAPTER 41

That evening, I made my way to the Volunteer Inn so the ghosts could search it for Black-Eye Elmore's treasure map. The inn was farther out of town, not far from the police station. Like the Swan, it was a white building with a slate roof. However, it was considerably larger, with rooms to rent. The sign outside showed a soldier dressed in a red army uniform from the Regency period. He looked very similar to Mr Wickers.

I'd never actually been inside the Volunteer, so I was nervous going in. I wasn't sure what to expect.

I opened the main door and was immediately hit by a wall of noise. About thirty mainly grey-haired male folk musicians were in the middle of playing a traditional folk tune, the speed of which seemed stupidly fast. Most held either guitars or mandolins, but I also recognised a dulcimer, a banjo and a ukulele.

It must be folk music night. I cursed myself for not checking the website.

I made my way to the bar and got served quickly, as everyone was playing or listening. Then I found a stool at the end of the bar. The ghosts set off on their hunt, and I laughed at Mr Darby in the distance, his hands over his ears. Clearly he didn't like folk music.

Eventually, the music stopped. There was a pause before the compère, who looked at least eighty-five, introduced the man next to him as a local folk star. The man nodded to the audience and began to strum his guitar. It was a slow number that sounded familiar. Then he started to sing.

A quiet voice spoke behind me. "Not seen you here before, love."

I turned and saw a woman aged about sixty, with grey hair and small round glasses. "No, it's my first time," I said. I held my hand out. "Trinity."

She shook it. "Margaret. What do you think?" She indicated the man singing.

"It's lovely." It really was.

"That's my husband. He wrote the song himself. He hardly puts that guitar down." She reached into her bag and pulled out a leaflet. "If you're interested, we're looking for more people to join the committee for the annual folk festival." She handed me the leaflet which I glanced at. *Your town needs you! Join the fight to save the folk festival.*

"Thanks. I'll have a read and think about it." I put the leaflet in my back pocket and continued listening to the music.

Just as the song finished, I felt a familiar tingle.

Lady Camilla appeared, floating over the crowd. "We think we've found the map!"

———

As the crowd clapped to Margaret's husband, I stood up and went into the ladies' so I could talk to Lady Camilla. Luckily it was empty.

Lady Camilla filled me in. "We've found the map. It's underneath a hearth stone in one of the guest bedrooms."

"You're sure?"

"Yes. But there's a problem."

My heart sank. There was always a problem. "What is it?"

"There's a ghost guarding it."

"What?"

"Are you deaf?" Lady Camilla scolded. "I said there's a ghost guarding it. She won't let us have the map."

"Can't you move it with magical powers?"

"No. Come up and see. The room is not occupied."

I followed Lady Camilla out of the toilet and upstairs to the rooms. She stopped outside number four and pointed at the lock.

It clicked open.

"Impressive," I said, and slipped in.

Mr Collingwood clicked his fingers and the lights came on. The other ghosts were there, too.

The room was cosy but modern, with a double bed, a TV in the corner and a dressing table. Lady Camilla pointed to the Victorian-style fireplace. In front was the hearth stone. "Is it under there?" I asked.

Lady Camilla nodded. "But this woman will not let us look at it or remove it." She pointed to a ghost half-hidden behind the others. Then they moved aside, and I saw the ghost in question.

She was only about five foot tall and wore an elaborate Georgian dress with a firm, straight bodice and skirts that went out sideways. On her head was a tall blonde wig with flowers dotted around it. Her face was powdered white, with a black beauty spot stuck on one of her cheeks.

This wasn't what I had expected at all. When Lady Camilla had said that a ghost was guarding the map, I'd expected a man, and a scary man at that.

She didn't move, so I stepped forward. "Hello, I'm Trinity. Trinity Bishop."

"Betsy Knight." She curtseyed.

"So, Betsy, how long have you been guarding Black-Eye's treasure map?"

"Since the second of November, 1798."

"Wow, that's a long time. Why are you guarding it?"

"No one may take the map from Black-Eye."

"But he's dead."

Betsy was silent.

"How did you come to guard the map?" I asked her.

"Black-Eye paid a witch handsomely to get me here. I was dying of pneumonia, and she trapped me in a locket and had me guard the map. I can't let you have the map unless you prove that you are Black-Eye's descendent by giving me the enchanted moonstone. Only then can I release the map." There was no emotion as she spoke.

I narrowed my eyes. "How can you stop me getting the map, though? I could just open up the hearth and take it."

Betsy stared at me. "I have powers to stop anyone taking it." She lifted her arms. Cold air rushed into the room, swirling and lifting me off the floor.

"All right!" I shouted.

Betsy lowered her arms and I came back down. It seemed she had the same powers as Lily.

"Right, so I have to come back with an enchanted moonstone. How do I get one of those?"

Betsy said nothing.

I sighed. At least we knew where the map was. Now I just had to find an enchanted moonstone and bring someone who was a direct descendant of Black-Eye.

CHAPTER 42

I n the evening, I sat on my sofa, Wentworth curled next to me. I stroked his head, but he was sleeping so soundly that he didn't stir.

He was all mine now. Aunt Ruby had popped in earlier with the adoption papers and I'd signed them. She had seemed rather smug, and I suspected that having me adopt Wentworth had been her aim all along. But I didn't care. He was safe now, and I intended to spoil him rotten.

"What are you doing?" said Lily next to me.

I jumped. "Don't sneak up on me! You know I don't like it."

Lily scowled at my phone. "You're always on that thing."

"I've been searching for something. And I think I've found it."

Lily clapped her hands. "Do tell!"

"Well, I got curious about how you all became ghosts. And seeing as none of you will tell me anything about it, I looked for myself."

Lily frowned and the other ghosts materialised, one by one. "She says she's found out how it happened," she told them.

"We heard," said Lady Camilla, sternly.

"It's all here, on the *National Newspaper Archive* website."

"The what?" Mr Darby asked.

"It's a website which stores scanned copies of historical newspapers. You pay a small fee, and then you can search newspapers from the past. I found out what happened."

The ghosts looked at each other. Lady Camilla lifted her chin. "Read it out, then."

I took a deep breath, and began.

"The Winchester Chronicle"
  "23rd April 1796"

"Dreadful Occurrence in Winchester."

"We have the solemn duty to relay a dreadful calamity that has transpired in the city of Winchester. An illustrious and well-attended Inn, known locally as the Jovial Huntsman, was consumed in an unforgiving fire on the 21st of this month.

"Amongst the lamented victims of this appalling event are the notable figures of Lady Camilla Du Borg and her nephew Mr Fitzroy Darby, both respected members of the nobility. Alongside them, we mourn the loss of Miss Lily Barrett, who was renowned for her congeniality and charm, aged just fifteen. Furthermore, we regret to report the untimely demise of the highly esteemed Reverend Collingwood, a respected clergyman under the patronage of Lady Camilla Du Borg. Reverend Collingwood was well-known for his wise counsel and benevolent disposition, serving his parish with great devotion and moral rectitude.

"In addition, the death of Mr Geoffrey Wickers, a

gentleman and a captain of substantial standing in the militia, further compounds the community's distress.

"Local eyewitnesses report that the fire swiftly engulfed the inn, leaving those within little chance of escape.

"Rescue efforts were immediately launched, but the severity of the fire rendered them futile. An investigation into the cause is underway, under the stewardship of local magistrates.

"As we reflect on this tragedy, we are reminded of the fleeting nature of our earthly existence and the importance of benevolence and goodwill to our fellow man. We implore our readers to hold the victims and their grieving families in their thoughts and prayers during this time of sorrow."

I swallowed, and tears welled up.

Lady Camilla floated over. "Now now, don't worry about us. We've all got over it. It would be nice to reach the afterlife one day, though. It's a little annoying to have been hanging around all this time."

Mr Wickers nodded. "No offence, but at some point I would like to move on."

"We all would," said Lady Camilla. "But if it had never happened, we never would have been immortalised in Jane Austen's book. She was the first ring-owner."

I wiped my eyes and looked at it on my finger, still amazed I had Jane Austen's actual ring, let alone what happened when I put it on. "You're loved all over the world by generations of people, and you will be for generations to come. Anyway, we'll find an enchanted moonstone and get the map. I'm determined to help you get to the afterlife. Not that I don't like you. In fact, I'm growing rather fond of you all."

Mr Darby bowed his head. "I admire your fortitude."

"Thank you. Maybe if you tell me how your connection to the ring came about…?"

"Now that we definitely can't tell you," said Lady Camilla, "because we don't know ourselves. What we do know is that one moment we were asleep in our beds, and the next we were ghosts who could only appear to the person wearing the ring."

"Never mind all that now," Lily interjected. "We can talk about it another day. For now, let's celebrate justice being done and Wentworth becoming a member of the family. He's so sweet." She went over and stroked him. He must have felt it, because he started purring.

"I'd like to celebrate by watching a wildlife programme on TV," said Mr Wickers.

"No, let's watch one of those films made of drawings that move," Lily said. "So clever."

I switched on the TV. "How about we watch one after the other?"

"Where are we going to sit?" asked Mr Wickers. "There's only two places to sit, what with Wentworth taking up a whole seat."

"I'm not kicking Wentworth off the chair—"

A knock on the door interrupted the squabbling. I got up and opened it.

It was O'Malley. Dressed casually in faded blue jeans, a black T-shirt and a day's worth of dark stubble, he looked more appealing than ever.

"Hello." I leaned against the door frame.

A warm glimmer flickered in his eyes. "I wondered how you were doing after the other day. Can I come in?"

"Sure." I opened the door wider.

He followed me into the living room, where the ghosts were still squabbling over what to watch on the TV. They fell silent when they saw O'Malley, except for Lily, who floated near him. "Ooh, DI Handsome," she cooed. "He can't stay away from you."

I gave her a hard stare. One by one, the ghosts went, leaving O'Malley and me alone.

"Take a seat." I indicated the chair opposite the sofa. Wentworth sat up, stretched, blinked at O'Malley, then flopped down and went back to sleep.

"Cute cat," O'Malley said, as he sat down.

"I've officially adopted him. He's friendly when he's not sleeping."

"So you're okay, after what happened?"

I wasn't okay, but I wasn't going to admit it. I decided I should show some British stiff upper lip. "I am, but thank you for checking. You didn't need to."

"I know. But I wanted to. I wanted to see you again."

I nodded, my expression neutral, though underneath I was trying not to get too hopeful that O'Malley was concerned beyond his duty as a police officer. "You're welcome to come into the tearoom any time."

"I know that, too. But maybe we could meet outside the tearoom?"

I stared at him. Was DI Handsome asking me out?

I heard Lily squeal in the kitchen. The ghosts were all listening in.

"I'd like that very much," I replied.

The End.

JANE AUSTEN AND ME

A long time ago, in late 1980s, when I was fifteen years old and in school, I was studying for my English literature exam and became very disillusioned with the study material that was forced upon me.

The books and plays were all about men, and the few women who were in them were either manipulative, stupid or passive observers of what men did.

The one glimmer of hope was when we were allowed to pick a literary book of our choice and write an essay on it. I'd no idea what to pick, as by that stage, I'd lost interest in reading for enjoyment.

Luckily, my mother had an idea: "Read *Pride and Prejudice* by Jane Austen; you'll love it." She gave me a brief outline. It sounded interesting so I bought a copy.

She was right. I read it, and loved it, then swiftly moved on to *Sense and Sensibility.* I loved them both because they were about women. And embarrassing family members. Yes, there were manipulative women in them, but there were also interesting and passionate women who were main characters, not afterthoughts.

What impressed me the most was that *Pride and Prejudice*

was set mainly in Hertfordshire, which was where I lived. So, for once, the material I was reading, although set over two hundred years before, felt relevant.

I wrote my essay comparing the relationship between the sisters in the two books, and got an A.

I've re-read *Pride and Prejudice* so many times since, I've lost count. I don't live in Hertfordshire anymore, but I do live close to Lyme Regis, where the infatuated Louisa Musgrove jumps from the Cobb and hurts herself.

I also live near Sidmouth, where I was delighted to find out that Jane Austen visited in 1801 and fell in love.

It was therefore only a matter of time before Jane Austen's work spilled over into my own.

ACKNOWLEDGMENTS

Many thanks to my husband for his unending support and love.

Also, to Liz Hedgecock, my editor, for her patience and assistance in getting this work out to you all.

Finally to my proofreader, Paula.

If you want to find out more about Jane Austen's visit to Sidmouth, you can download a fact sheet about it by signing up to my newsletter as well as a recipe for Devon Apple Cake:

www.suzybussell.com / tearoom

Book 2 in the series is available to pre-order here:

Festivals, Fears and Fatalities
Trinity and the ghosts are back!

It's the Sidmouth Annual Folk Festival and when the head of the festival is brutally murdered, Trinity and the ghosts must work out who the killer is.

Trinity also has her own quest to help the ghosts find the enchanted moonstone to help them get to the afterlife.

Printed in Great Britain
by Amazon